"Still playing the field, Reid?"

"Something wrong with that?"

"Of course not. You're a free man now."

"No second thoughts, Annys?"

"Have you?" she asked incredulously.

There was a heartbeat's silence. "Some. I'm still powerfully attracted to you. And it isn't all one-sided, either."

She made an impatient gesture of dismissal, and he said, "Don't belittle it. Sex has made the world go round since the beginning of time. It's what marriage is based on, after all."

"Maybe for you—"

"You hardly knew me when you agreed to marry me. You wanted me, and you didn't give a thought to the other things marriage involved—"

DAPHNE CLAIR lives in Aotearoa—New Zealand—with her Dutch-born husband. Their five children have left home but drift back at irregular intervals. At eight years old she embarked on her first novel, about taming a tiger. Although this epic never reached a publisher, metamorphosed male tigers still prowl the pages of her romances. Her other writing includes nonfiction, poetry and short stories, and Daphne has won literary prizes in New Zealand and America.

Books by Daphne Clair

Daphne *Clair*

Flame on the Horizon

Harlequin Books

TORONTO • NEW YORK • LONDON
AMSTERDAM • PARIS • SYDNEY • HAMBURG
STOCKHOLM • ATHENS • TOKYO • MILAN
MADRID • WARSAW • BUDAPEST • AUCKLAND

ISBN 0-373-11648-9

FLAME ON THE HORIZON

Copyright © 1993 by Daphne de Jong.

CHAPTER ONE

IF ANNYS had known that Reid Bannerman was booked for the voyage, nothing would have induced her to board the Toroa.

It was bad luck that her car had a flat that morning when she went to throw her kit into it. The wheel nuts were locked tight, and it took her longer than it should have to change the tyre. After which she surveyed the dusty knees and oil-streaked top of her sky-blue silk-look tracksuit—a new design boldly displaying her own logo—and realised she'd have to change.

Reluctant to unpack her kit, which contained some very smart casual wear that she'd hoped would constitute discreet advertising, she'd taken time to find a pair of jeans that would pass, and a purple sweatshirt that looked reasonably decent. They wouldn't make the impression she'd hoped for but she had no time now to worry about that.

She was confident of making up the twenty minutes easily on the four-hour journey north between Auckland and the Bay of Islands, but was further delayed by a truck that had lost its load of kiwi fruit on the winding road over the Brynderwyn Hills, south of Whangarei.

Calm down, she told herself as she helped the driver and his mate retrieve broken boxes and return them to the truck, and clear piles of ruined fuzzy green fruit to the side of the road. She glanced at her watch and took several deep breaths to still a rising panic. Proof, she realised, that she needed this break from the business.

'Not my idea of a holiday,' her friend and assistant Kate Driver had said. 'You mean you *pay* to be allowed to haul on ropes and set sails and—whatever you do to make sailing ships go? Sounds like a gigantic con to me. If you're crewing, shouldn't they pay *you*?'

'An adventure cruise is a learning experience,' Annys pointed out. 'They take on amateurs as crew, and teach them how to sail a three-master. And it's not just sailing all the time. We land at various places on the coast, do some hiking and diving, spend time on several islands, and try rock-climbing, rafting——'

Kate moaned. 'You need a *rest*, woman! You'll come back even more exhausted than you are!'

Annys laughed. 'It'll be a change from drawing designs and talking to buyers and doing the accounts. I'd go mad just lying on some beach, or eating myself sick on a luxury liner.'

'It would do me. You're so *physical*, Annys!' Kate was an excellent saleswoman and a very capable manager, but her interest in sport was purely as a spectator.

'Big business corporations send their junior executives on adventure voyages, you know,' Annys told her. 'Character-building. It's supposed to increase resourcefulness and initiative. Maybe I'll send you when I come back, if I think it worthwhile.'

Kate shuddered. 'My character's had all the building it needs, thanks. And you're not short on resourcefulness and initiative, either,' she observed. 'How old are you? Twenty-nine,' she answered herself. 'And the owner of a chain of sportswear boutiques that's known throughout New Zealand and now exporting to the States and Europe—all done in five years, working all kinds of hours without a break. No wonder your doctor told you to take a holiday. But I'm still not sure that he meant what you have in mind!'

By the time Annys had garaged her car at a friend's house in the little tourist town of Russell and got a lift to the wharf, the Toroa's crew was just about to raise the gangway. She had no trouble identifying the tall ship, a nineteenth-century anachronism with its masts towering over the sleek sea-going modern yachts and cabin cruisers in the bay.

'Miss Sherwood?' asked a young Maori man, his brown skin a stunning contrast to a spanking white T-shirt with a picture of the albatross for which the Toroa was named blazoned on the front. 'We'd given you up. Let me carry that.' He had taken a quick inventory of her tall, lithe figure, clear hazel eyes and shining brown hair tied back with a scarf, as she'd raced towards him, and obviously decided he liked the result.

'Sorry!' she gasped as he took her pack. 'Thanks. I had a puncture first thing this morning, and then got held up on the road.'

'Well, glad you made it. I'm Tony, the first mate.'

'Hi, Tony. My name's Annys.'

He dumped her pack on the deck and helped to bring the gangway up. 'Do you want someone to show you down to the women's quarters now, or would you rather wait until we leave the harbour?'

'I'll wait,' Annys said. 'I don't want to miss any of this. We don't start helping to work the ship yet, I take it?'

He laughed. 'Just keep out of the way and enjoy the view,' he advised. 'In a couple of days we'll have you all working like galley-slaves. Most of the guest voyagers have introduced themselves already, but we'll do it formally later.'

She ought to go and say hello to some of the people leaning on the rails or gathered in a group on top of the deckhouse, get to know some of her fellow voyagers. But she needed time to calm down and unwind after her hectic dash. She turned instead to watch the wharf slide away, and the anchored pleasure boats, and the town strung along the shingly beach and climbing into the low hills dusted with white-flowered manuka scrub.

Crew members climbed into the rigging and let the sails go from their ropes with a whoosh, and when the wind filled the canvas she felt a leap of pure pleasure as the ship gathered speed and swayed, moving like a living creature beneath her feet.

Peering over the rail, she saw the blue water rippling against the timbers and curling back in a white lip. Looking aft, she watched the wake widening behind them, and a gull swooping down to the water and up again to soar above the masts.

That brought her eyes back to the sailors in the rigging, climbing nimbly down the ratlines now.

'Think you can do that?' Tony had come to stand beside her, grinning as he asked the question.

'I don't see why not,' Annys answered him. She was nervous of heights but not terrified. And she always responded to a challenge.

'Good for you.' He put a hand briefly on her shoulder and went forward to speak to one of the crew.

They were still in the harbour, but the land on either side was getting further away. Historic Russell, once notorious throughout the Pacific when it was called Kororareka and was a gathering place for whalers and traders and maybe the first land that rough and ready sailors had touched on in months, huddled between the hills and the water. Nearly two hundred years ago the port would have been crowded with tall sailing ships like the Toroa, from England, America, France, even Russia.

Directly opposite was Paihia, then a mission station and now a thriving tourist centre with motels, hotels, and souvenir shops competing for the visitors' attention. People still came to the Bay of Islands from all over the world, a few by sea in luxury liners, but most by air at least as far as Auckland, the journey taking just hours instead of months.

On a tiny island just out of Russell she could see the distinctive signs of long-ago Maori habitation, the terraces that would once have been surmounted by high fences and backed by deep ditches, so that the resident tribe could defend itself against a marauding enemy.

The ship slid past Flagstaff Hill, where in the turbulent 1840s the chief Hone Heke had four times chopped down the symbol of British sovereignty, and many years afterwards his descendants had helped to erect a replacement as a gesture of reconciliation.

Soon the ship had passed the headland and entered the outer bay. Later a voice on the ship's intercom told them they were passing Motuarohia, where Captain Cook on his voyage of discovery had made his first landing in the Bay of Islands. It was also known as Roberton Island, scene of an ancient tragedy when a Mrs

Roberton and her children and manservant had been murdered there.

More cheerfully, the voice went on to tell them that there were about two hundred islands in the Bay. They were now passing Motukiekie where plantings of majestic, symmetrical Norfolk pine made a contrast to the supple native climber and other plants more common to these islands. And the larger one coming up was Urupukapuka, a popular island for camping and picnicking. Annys could see several inviting-looking coves with white, sandy beaches.

They had left Urupukapuka behind when there was a cry of excitement from the group on the galley roof, and at the same instant Annys saw a school of dolphins leaping and cavorting in the wake. They played about for several minutes before disappearing in a series of speeding shadows far down in the water.

She was still smiling at the unexpected sight when a deep, even voice said, 'Hello, Annys. I thought it was you.'

No! Her head whipped round, the smile abruptly wiped from her mouth, her heart giving a lurch of stupid fright. She stared into dark, green-flecked eyes, then stepped back, instinctively glancing towards the land they had left behind.

'It's too far to swim,' Reid pointed out. 'And I don't think they'd lower a boat to take you back.'

They would if it was an emergency, she thought. They could send a helicopter, couldn't they? Or something . . .

She could say she was sick, feign appendicitis, food poisoning, anything.

No, she couldn't. Sanity took hold. Of course she wouldn't do that, put a lot of people to so much trouble and expense just because she found herself on a ship with a man who...

A man she couldn't stand to be with. And what was he doing here, anyway? That thought she put into words. 'What the *hell* are you doing here?'

She hadn't meant to sound so furious, so shaken. But the vehemence in her voice made him raise his almost-black brows. He'd had time to control his own surprise, obviously. She wondered how long ago he'd spotted her. When she'd come on board, flushed and flustered and definitely not looking her best?

He said calmly, 'The same as you, I suppose.'

'I'm surprised you could spare the time.'

'Ditto,' he said crisply. 'I'm doing a trial run, to see if I think it's worthwhile to invest in adventure cruises for my staff members.' He paused, while she digested that. His staff must have increased considerably. 'You've been pretty busy yourself, these last few years.'

And successful. She hoped he knew how successful. 'I was due for a break,' she said. Some break! With Reid on board, she'd end up more strung out than ever at the end of the month. A whole three weeks in his company didn't bear thinking of.

They would touch on land, though. She could leave then, tell them she didn't think cruising was for her after all, she was going to fly to the Cook Islands instead. Or Hawaii, Alaska, Siberia—anywhere to get away from Reid Bannerman.

'Me too,' Reid said. 'I need one.'

She looked at him properly for the first time. His hair was as dark and thick as ever, the wind blowing it over his forehead, and he was still built like an athlete, with no signs of flabbiness. There were more pronounced lines about his eyes, and something different about his mouth, a grimness that hadn't been there before.

Returning her stare, he said, 'You haven't changed.'

It should have been a compliment, but she had the feeling he was talking about more than the way she looked, and that he'd wanted her to be changed.

Without thinking, she said, 'You look older.'

'I am older,' he pointed out.

'So am I.' With some confused idea of making amends, she added, 'You've no need to flatter me.'

'I wasn't. You look just the same.'

'Well, I'm not.' The years had changed her. She was harder, less vulnerable now. Tough. She didn't need any man to validate her existence. Maybe she ought to be grateful to Reid for that.

Reid was looking thoughtful now, his eyes making a deliberate, slow inspection of her. Her body prickled with awareness, with anger. She stiffened, standing straighter. When his eyes returned to her face, lingering a moment on her mouth, she said, 'Have you quite finished?'

'I stand by my opinion.'

'That's typically male! Appearance is everything!'

'I said,' he pointed out, 'you *look* just the same. So far I've no cause to think you've changed in any other way, either.'

Annys clutched the rail with her right hand to stop it coming up and slapping him, a dead give-away that he'd riled her into a temper. She'd always had a low flash-point where Reid was concerned. He could make her angrier than anyone she'd ever known, but the reverse side was the passion that he had roused in her, some-times with just a look, a word . . .

Her lips parted involuntarily at the memory, her gaze caught by his. She saw the dilation of his pupils, the tautness in his expression, and knew that he could read her expression just as she read his.

'God!' he said, sounding as appalled as Annys felt. 'That, too!'

'No,' Annys said, denying the undeniable, her voice scarcely audible. She shook her head. 'No, Reid!'

'Don't worry,' he said, his voice harsh and low. 'I've no intention of falling into that trap again.'

Then he turned and left her standing there. She watched him stride to the stern rail, where he placed his hands wide apart on broad polished wood and stood with his back to her until she wrenched her gaze away and forced herself to walk in the opposite direction.

She picked up her bag and took it down to the women's cabin amidships. It wasn't hard to find, and she noted the only bunk—a lower one—that didn't have belongings on it proclaiming ownership, and sat down.

There must be a way out of this, she thought, trying to recall the itinerary. When did they reach the mainland again? Not for about ten days, 'depending on weather conditions and the captain's discretion', the printed sheet had said. Surely she could survive ten days? They weren't the only people on board, after all. There were nine regular crew and two dozen paying ones. Thirty other people to talk to, people she could place between her and Reid. She needn't even speak to him. And as he obviously felt the same...

No problem, she told herself; they both wanted to avoid each other. Stop panicking, because that was what this shaking, damp-palmed adrenalin rush was. Relax and enjoy yourself. It's what you're here for.

And nothing, certainly not Reid Bannerman, was going to interfere with that.

It took an effort, though, to make herself go up on deck again. She might have remained skulking in the cabin, except that one of the other women came in and saw her.

'Hi!' She was about twenty-five, a solid young woman with short sand-coloured hair, wearing shorts and a thin sleeveless top. 'It's getting cool up there,' she said in a soft North American accent. 'I came to fetch a sweat-shirt. You're not sick, are you?'

Annys shook her head and stood up. 'Do I look sick?'

'A bit pale, but maybe you're always like that. Some people are. I'm Jane Finch. I saw you come on board.'

'Annys Sherwood.' She explained briefly again about the disastrous morning.

Jane laughed. 'You were lucky to get here.'

Was I? Annys thought grimly. Maybe someone was trying to tell me something, and I should have listened.

'Coming up on deck?' Jane asked, pulling a sweater out of a large khaki backpack. 'I'll introduce you to some of the others.'

'Yes,' Annys answered decisively. There was safety in numbers. 'Thank you.'

Reid was still standing at the rail, and that fact made it difficult for Annys to concentrate on the introduc-tions. But she settled in among the group on the deckhouse roof. Soon she was chatting to a middle-aged woman who said she'd always wanted to go on a sailing voyage but had never got the chance until her children left home and her husband offered this one as a birthday present, and a fortyish man who was a writer researching for a novel set in the nineteenth century.

His name was Tancred Withers, he told her hopefully, but she'd never heard of him. His hair was expensively cut to disguise an incipient bald patch, and he wore designer jeans and a Pierre Cardin shirt with several buttons open to discreetly expose what Annys suspected was a salon-tanned chest. The effect was one of studied casualness.

He rather fancied himself, but was entertaining to talk with, showing a dry wit that Annys enjoyed. And she liked the fact that, although his interest had been obvious when Jane had introduced her, he had simply courteously included her in the conversation he'd been having with the woman who'd described herself as a housewife, rather than transferred his attention, as some men might have. When she laughed at something he said, she saw Reid's head twitch, his shoulders tense. A little later he moved, turning to rest back against the rail to one side of the bow with his arms folded, studiously looking at everything but the group on the roof.

Annys pushed back a strand of hair that the wind had loosened, and leaned closer to hear something Tancred said, exchanged some remarks with others in the group, and managed to ignore Reid's silent, aloof presence until lunchtime.

Lunch was served on deck, buffet-style at a long folding table. Annys helped herself to salad, an avocado and a boiled egg, and Tancred Withers poised a jug of mayonnaise over her plate, inviting her to, 'Say when.'

A decisive voice said, 'She doesn't like the stuff.'

Reid was standing across the table from them. As Annys looked up at him, he clamped his lips shut as though annoyed with himself, and Tancred said into the small silence, 'You know each other?' Then, 'Silly question. Obviously you do.'

And Reid said clearly, deliberately, 'You might say that. As a matter of fact, we used to be married to each other.'

CHAPTER TWO

ANNYS hastily righted the plate that was tipping in her hand. She wanted to throw it at Reid, to yell, How dare you?

But that would have added even more piquancy for the onlookers. The electric silence was as loud as a shout. Everyone seemed to be staring at them.

Her cheeks burned with anger, and there was a buzzing in her ears. Reid was looking at her, meeting her furious gaze with a challenging glare, his lips curved slightly in what she decided was a sneer. And there wasn't a thing she could say.

Tancred gave an embarrassed little laugh. 'Really?' he said weakly. He glanced at the jug of mayonnaise in his hand and put it down on the table. 'Well...'

Everyone else seemed to come to life, turning discreetly away to concentrate on the food, talking animatedly to their neighbours.

Annys said clearly, not too loudly, 'It was a long time ago.'

Reid lifted his brows. 'Not so long...'

Tancred said, 'Oh? And did you know, when you booked this cruise——?'

'No.' Annys was still looking at Reid. 'It was just an unfortunate coincidence.'

'Well—er—too bad,' Tancred murmured, obviously torn between embarrassment and curiosity. Annys supposed that this would be great material for a writer.

Reid glanced at him impatiently. 'We'll just have to make the best of it,' he said. 'Won't we, Annys? I'm sure we can manage to be civilised for the duration of the voyage.'

A lot more easily if you hadn't told everyone, she accused him silently. This wasn't the time and place for a boiling row, but he needn't think he was going to get away with it, she promised herself. What was the matter with him anyway? Reid wasn't the type to go broadcasting his private business to a bunch of perfect strangers.

Deliberately she turned away from him and said to Tancred, 'Let's sit somewhere and enjoy our lunch. It certainly looks delicious.'

She was sure she could feel Reid's eyes on her as she and Tancred walked to a sun-warmed bulkhead and sat down with their backs to it. She studiously ate everything on her plate and even commented on how good it tasted, but it might as well have been sawdust and ashes. Reid was out of sight, she discovered on covertly glancing around, but she was acutely conscious that he could reappear at any moment.

Tancred was saying something she had been too busy brooding to hear.

'Sorry?'

'Sweets,' he said. 'Do you want some?'

Annys shook her head. 'Just coffee. I'll get it.'

When he insisted she let him, though. If she stayed here she wouldn't bump into Reid. She could do with a breathing space before she had to deal with him again.

Late in the afternoon the ship approached one of the smaller islands and came to anchor in a tranquil cove.

The water was clear as glass right down to the seabed. Hermit crabs crawled lazily across a carpet of broken shells and coloured pebbles, and a school of tiny glittering fish darted above them like moving sunlight and then were gone. Beyond a strip of white sand, birds called from hills covered with spreading puriri, tall taraire, glossy dark green taupata, and feathery ponga ferns with silver-backed leaves.

Captain Walsh, a stocky, weathered man with a salt-and-pepper beard whose appearance spelled out solid reliability, announced that the swimming was good here, and those who wanted to could go ashore by dinghy. 'No cigarettes or matches,' he warned. 'No fires on the island. Dinner is on board, and afterwards we'll outline tomorrow's programme for you.'

Annys, Jane and most of the other women changed in the narrow cabin lined with bunks, good-naturedly making room for one another, and back on deck plunged into the clear salt water. About half a dozen passengers had elected to take the dinghy ashore, but a quick glance showed Annys that Reid wasn't among them.

She looked back at the ship, and saw him poised on the rail, ready to dive. As he bent forward and arrowed into the water she couldn't help a tug of sheer pleasure at the masculine grace of his body entering the water with barely a splash. She turned to swim away, well off from the ship and the other swimmers cavorting about near the hull. Some time she was going to confront Reid, but it needed to be when she could be sure of a reasonable amount of privacy.

After working off some energy doing a fast crawl back and forth across the bay, she swam more slowly to the shore, where the dinghy sat on the sand, its occupants having disappeared into the trees. Looking back over the water, she thought she could make out Reid's black head, slightly apart from the others. Some had climbed back on board, but Tancred was swimming in leisurely fashion towards her, pausing to wave. Good manners demanded that she wait for him.

He splashed ashore, dressed in briefs featuring a startling zigzag pattern, and casting an admiring glance over her sleek wine-red suit, cut high at the sides and low at the back.

'This is the life,' he said, sauntering towards her. His arm lifted as though he would drape it about her, but she casually moved away, and he let it drop.

'Tony said we'll be working like galley-slaves after today,' she said as their feet sank into the soft, gritty sand.

'Tony?'

'The mate.'

'Oh, yes.' He stopped beside her, getting his breath, and turned to look at the ship. 'I'm out of condition. Ought to get more exercise.'

'I thought I might climb up there.' She indicated the steep, bush-covered slope behind them. 'Want to come?'

'Sure.' He turned and surveyed the hill. 'Why not?'

There was a path of sorts, winding up between moss-covered trees, sometimes so steep that steps had been cut in the hillside. About halfway up they met two people coming down again.

'Is it worth it?' Tancred panted.

'Wonderful view.'

He grunted. 'Better be.'

Ahead of him, Annys laughed. She stopped, looking back. 'Are you OK?'

'I'm fine,' he assured her. Then he grinned, adding, 'But obviously I'm not as fit as you are. The view from here isn't half bad either.' His eyes teased.

'Stop ogling, Tancred,' Annys advised him without rancour.

He laughed, and there was a smile on her face as she returned to the climb. She had dealt with his sort before, frankly male chauvinist but gallant with it, and harmless. In small doses they could be fun, provided the boundaries were spelled out for them.

They reached the top and discovered a cleared plateau. Several of their party were taking photographs or lounging on the ground. Annys and Tancred joined them, sitting side by side near the edge where the trees had been cut back to allow an unimpeded view of a shining sea smudged with misty islands. The sun was beginning to set, and they could see the ship below them, taking on a faint pink glow. The water turned from silver to gold, and the desultory conversations among the watchers died by tacit consent into a spellbound silence as the sun hovered on the horizon and then sank with surprising speed, a disc of fire leaving a fading bronze polish on the sea.

'We'd better get down that path before it gets dark,' someone said, and everyone began to move.

'Coming?' Tancred asked Annys.

'Soon,' she answered. 'You go ahead.'

He could hardly refuse. Reluctantly he joined the others who were now chattering on their way down the hill.

Reid's voice said, 'Tired of him already?'

Annys wasn't sure at what point she had known he was there. But before the others had left his presence had been tangible to her. She could feel his gaze now, her bare back tingling in awareness.

She stood up slowly, and turned to face him. Like her, he had swum ashore, and he was wearing only briefs. More conservative than Tancred's, they were plain solid black, but fitted like skin, emphasising his maleness, accentuating the width of his chest and length of his lean, muscled legs.

'I'm not tired of him,' she said. 'He's a very pleasant man.' Ignoring the disbelieving sound that he made, she went on, 'But I wanted to talk to you.'

Reid's eyes narrowed warily. 'About?'

'About that gratuitous announcement you made at lunch,' she told him, the anger that had been dissipated by a long swim and a restful sunset rising again. 'Why on earth did you take it upon yourself to tell the whole world about our... our private affairs?'

'Our marriage,' he said flatly.

'Our divorce,' Annys amended. 'It concerns no one but us, and they didn't know anything about it until you gratuitously broadcast the fact. That's the way I'd have preferred it to stay, and I'd have thought that you would, too.'

She thought his jaw tightened fractionally. 'Why so anxious? Someone waiting in the wings?'

'No one is waiting in the wings, as you put it. I just don't want to be coupled in any way with you! And there was absolutely no need for these people to know anything about our—previous relationship.'

For a moment he was silent, and she wondered if he was thinking up an excuse or marshalling arguments. 'I thought,' he said finally, 'that it was better that way.

There are bound to be undercurrents between us. They're going to notice, and speculate.'

'You had no right to take it upon yourself to inform them! If we just stayed out of each other's way, no one would have noticed——'

'Of course they would. Communal living does that. Relationships are intense, and everyone notices any tensions between members of the group. This way will prevent a lot of gossip and misunderstanding. They all know now that we've a previous—unhappy—association, and they'll stay out of it.'

'It wasn't always unhappy,' Annys said involuntarily. Immediately she wanted to recall the words.

'No,' he said slowly. 'Regrets, Annys?'

'Of course I have regrets,' she said. 'That doesn't mean I want to change anything. Like you, I have no intention of repeating previous mistakes.'

'So, it's just as well that the people we're going to be living with for the next three weeks are aware that it's no use expecting us to play Happy Families, isn't it?'

'That's your opinion. Did it occur to you I might have a different one, that I had a right to be consulted?'

'I thought it would ultimately save us some embarrassment——'

'*Save* us embarrassment?' Her voice rose scornfully. 'Do you think I wasn't embarrassed when you came out with that bald announcement at lunch?'

'You were angry,' he answered. 'That's different.'

Was it? But she wasn't going to allow him that point. 'Because you'd embarrassed me,' she argued. 'Of course I was angry. What the hell did you expect?'

'I've never known what to expect from you, Annys,' he said. 'That's what makes you so...'

'What?' she demanded as he paused. 'Difficult to live with?' He hadn't been able to live with her in the end, nor she with him. Although at the finish other factors had come into it. 'I'm not the only one,' she reminded him.

'I was going to say—exciting,' he drawled. 'But I wouldn't want you to misconstrue.'

He wouldn't want her to think of it as a compliment, he meant. He might have liked excitement when they'd first met, but it had soon palled.

But by the way he was looking at her now, as though he had just become aware of how little she was wearing, it seemed exciting had its momentary attractions. Suddenly she was conscious that they were alone here, no one within calling distance. And her body was responding to his intent gaze, her thin, clinging swimsuit in the gathering dusk doing nothing to disguise it.

A tui called seductively from the bush, half a dozen notes in a full-throated contralto, and then was silent. Abruptly, Annys moved, determined to break the spell that threatened to weave its well-remembered web. 'It's getting dark,' she said. 'I'm going back.'

He followed her as she plunged down the path. A couple of times she slipped where it was very steep, grabbing at saplings and protruding roots to stop herself from falling.

He said sharply, 'Slow down, Annys. You'll have an accident!' But she ignored him and kept on going.

Reid swore and came after her, capturing her wrist, bringing her to a jarring halt. 'I said, slow down!'

She pulled away. 'You don't tell me what to do, Reid! Not any more.' She went on climbing down, missed her footing and slid a few feet before righting herself, clinging to the rough bark of a kahikatea that swayed with her weight.

As she released it and stood alone, Reid caught up with her, his hands closing over her upper arms, jerking her round to face him. 'Someone has to! You'll hurt yourself, and they'll have to send out a rescue party! Have some sense, Annys! What are you running from—me?'

Her head lifted, her hands pushing against him. 'I'm not frightened of you!'

'No?' he said tautly. His hold tightened, bringing her closer to him, their bodies touching. 'No,' he repeated in a different tone. 'It isn't me you're frightened of, is it?'

They were too close. She felt the slick warmth of his bare chest against her palms, and stared into his eyes, her skin suddenly hot in spite of the cool evening shade under the trees. Everything had gone very quiet.

'No wonder you're scared,' Reid murmured, staring back at her, his lips only inches away from hers. 'I'm bloody terrified, myself.'

Annys stood still, not daring to move. She tried to breathe normally, to keep the flare of desire out of her eyes. Scarcely opening her lips, she said, 'Let me go, Reid.'

He wrenched his eyes away from hers to look up at the pale sky beyond the trees, taking a deep, shaking breath. Then he stepped away as far as the narrow, steep path allowed. 'You always did pack a punch, Annys.'

I'm not the only one, she thought. She said, her voice brittle with the effort to keep it steady, 'I'll thank you to keep your hands to yourself in future.'

He gave an odd little laugh that was almost a groan. 'You can count on it. Break your lovely neck if you want to. I swear I won't touch a hair of your head. Let's get out of here.'

Annys turned again to forge her way downhill. But she forced herself to slow down, because he was right. There was no sense in risking an accident and possible injury. And he had just promised not to touch her, hadn't he? So there was nothing to run away from.

They were the last back on board, and to her annoyance Annys noticed a few covertly interested glances coming their way. She went straight down to the women's cabin and changed into a lightly padded dark green tracksuit, glamorous but warm. Mindful of the notice asking users to conserve water, she brushed out the tangles in her hair without rinsing it, and tied it back again. She had just time to use a lip gloss and brush a subtle shadow on her eyelids before the sound of a brass bell signalled dinner.

It was taken at two long tables below decks. Annys was careful not to choose the same one that Reid did and she sat with her back to him. There were other Americans besides Jane, and one man with a thick German-sounding accent tried to talk with two giggling Japanese girls. Annys discovered that the man sitting near her was an accountant, one woman a bus driver and another owned a small publishing business. Tancred, seated to the other side of Annys, pricked up his ears at that and turned to engage the woman in deep discussion.

Annys smiled at the striking olive-skinned brunette opposite her whose face looked rather familiar. 'What do you do?'

'I act,' the woman said. 'I'm Xianthe Andrews.'

'Of course. You've been on TV. Ever since I saw you at lunch, I've been trying to figure out where I knew you from.' Only she'd been too busy feeling furious with Reid to put her mind to it. 'One somehow doesn't expect to see TV stars turn up in real life.'

Xianthe smiled. She was a stunner, Annys thought. She appeared to be wearing no make-up but still looked great. 'I guess,' she agreed. 'Though I'm hardly a star yet. What do you do?'

'Design sportswear,' Annys said. 'And sell it.'

Xianthe inspected the logo on Annys's tracksuit top and exclaimed, 'You're Annys of Annys Leisurewear! I *love* your stuff! It looks great and it's so comfortable and practical. I'm wearing one of your jackets!' She held out her hands to display the zip-fronted garment, soft blue with pink and pale green accents.

'I noticed,' Annys assured her, smiling her appreciation.

Jane, the American girl who was sitting further along, caught the conversation and joined in. 'You designed that? Wow, that's gorgeous! Where could I buy something like that?'

'I'll give you a card later,' Annys promised, 'with a list of my sportswear boutiques and some other stores that stock my designs.'

Over cups of coffee Captain Walsh, at the head of the other table, called for silence and stood up to outline the programme for the next day.

'We stay anchored here for another day,' he told them. 'In that time we'll go over safety procedures more thoroughly——'

Tancred leaned over to whisper in her ear, 'You missed that yesterday.'

Annys nodded, and then looked back to the captain, on the way her glance colliding with a dark, hostile stare from Reid. She lifted her chin and kept her gaze raptly on Captain Walsh.

'We've let you off easy today,' he was saying. 'Tomorrow you all become real sailors, and shirkers can expect to be keel-hauled.'

He let the laughter die before outlining the duties the part-time sailors could expect to be detailed for. 'Galley duty helping the cook, polishing the brass fittings, housekeeping tasks, swabbing decks and of course working the ship.' He paused. 'There's no division of duties by sex. You'll be formed into watches, and so that we get a fairly good balance of age, ability and sexes the first mate and I have drawn up those from the information you gave on your application forms. Lists will be posted on the mast, together with a rough schedule,' he added, indicating the mainmast in the centre of the long cabin. 'One more thing. No one is obliged to go aloft and set the sails. The crew will show you what to do if you choose to volunteer. Tomorrow we'll give you a chance to practise while the ship's at anchor. And no one is to try it without a safety harness. Breakfast's at seven tomorrow. We recommend a swim before it.' Amid laughter and groans, he asked, 'Any questions?'

There were a few, and then he called for volunteers to help clear the tables. Nearly everyone did, making quick work of it, and a few stayed to help wash up while the others dispersed about the ship.

Some went for a swim in the dark. Annys thought about it but changed her mind when she saw Reid strip off his shirt with quick, impatient movements and dive into the blackness. He came up some way from the ship, and swam so far towards the open sea that she found herself clutching the rail and watching with aching eyes the faint white gleam that was the rise and fall of his arms powering through the water.

When he finally turned and came back, she waited until he was only yards from the side and then stepped back and almost ran down to the cabin. Otherwise she wasn't sure she wouldn't have screamed at him the minute he climbed back on board, What do you think you were doing, swimming out so far? Where were you trying to go—South America?

And of course it was none of her business. She didn't have the right any more to question his actions—not that she ever had questioned them, not aloud—and she certainly didn't need to worry about him. Reid had always been more than capable of taking care of himself.

CHAPTER THREE

DISMAYED, Annys gazed at the piece of paper pinned to the mast. She'd told herself it wouldn't happen, but it had. Her name and Reid's were on the same watch list, under Tony Hiwi, the first mate.

She was wearing her swimsuit, ready for the early morning dip recommended by Captain Walsh, pausing on her way out to read the lists.

'I'll swap,' she told herself as she climbed the narrow companionway to the deck. 'Someone will be willing to exchange with me.'

Several men were in the water. She recognised Tony and a couple of other staff members, and thought the others were guest voyagers. Reid wasn't among them, and she was breathing a sigh of relief when his voice just behind her said, 'Having second thoughts, Annys?'

'No,' she said, casting him a scornful look and, discarding the towel about her shoulders, climbed on to the rail.

He was right beside her, and they dived in perfect unison, coming up to a chorus of congratulatory cheers from the other swimmers. The water was very cold but exhilarating.

'Beautiful timing,' Tony called to them. 'That was a picture to watch.'

'It seems we're the star turn,' Reid murmured, pushing wet hair away from his eyes and waving an acknowledgement to their audience. 'We always were good together.'

She ignored him. 'Coincidence,' she told Tony, and turned to swim away.

This time Reid kept pace with her. 'Sleep all right?' he asked her when she finally slowed down.

Annys blinked. Why was he making inane conversation? 'Fine,' she answered shortly. She had finally, after lying awake for hours reliving a past she had thought put behind her.

She wasn't going to ask him how he'd slept, she decided. But he told her anyway. 'I didn't,' he said, floating beside her, his arms moving lazily. 'Your friend Tancred snores.'

She didn't know what she was supposed to say to that. She turned over, and began a fast backstroke towards the ship.

Reid stayed alongside her easily, using a strong, leisurely crawl. Annys was groping for the rope ladder to help her up the side when he said, 'We're on the same watch, did you know?'

'I know. I intend to ask for an exchange.'

He found the ladder before she did, and hung on to it with one hand, facing her. 'Good,' he said. 'Because if you hadn't, I would.'

The quick stab of hurt she felt was stupid. They'd agreed to keep out of each other's way, hadn't they? She reached past him to grasp the ladder, and the movement combined with the rocking of the ship brought them into contact, legs brushing together.

Clumsily, she thrashed against him, trying to get away, and lost her hold on the ladder, briefly sinking. She surfaced, gasping, and Reid shot out a hand to her, his fingers closing over her arm.

'Steady!' he said in a low voice. And then, 'I could scarcely rape you here, even if I wanted to.'

'I just lost my grip,' she said. 'There's no need to be snide. Are you going to use that damn ladder, or can I?'

He pushed away from the side. 'Be my guest.'

'Thank you.' This time she took a firm hold on the wet rope and in moments was over the side, picking up her towel. Jane, emerging from the companionway, saw her shiver and asked, 'Cold, is it?'

'Mmm, but great,' Annys assured her.

A warm shower would have been good, but it was a luxury not available on board. Instead she dressed in trousers and a wool sweater, and then went to see if she could find the mate.

'It's not me, is it?' Tony asked when she explained what she wanted.

Annys shook her head. 'Of course not.' The crew had mostly been occupied yesterday when Reid had made his shock announcement. Maybe Tony hadn't heard about it. As surely Captain Walsh hadn't, or he wouldn't have been so tactless as to put her and Reid on the same watch. 'I'd feel happier in another watch, that's all,' she ended lamely.

'The captain's not keen on altering the watches,' Tony told her dubiously. 'They've all been carefully worked out for balance, and once people start swapping about we can end up with a lot of light, small people in one watch that makes it hard for them to handle some of the ropes. That's not just inconvenient; in a crisis it can be downright dangerous.'

'If I find someone of about my build, then,' Annys suggested.

'I could talk to him, I suppose,' Tony said. 'You know, if you've taken a dislike to someone, those things often work themselves out in the course of the voyage. It's amazing what happens when people find themselves in a situation where they have to co-operate and rely on each other.'

If she and Reid hadn't managed to co-operate in two years of living together, she wanted to tell him, they weren't likely to manage it in three weeks. 'You don't understand the problem,' she told him. 'It's more complicated than that.'

'You're not being harassed, are you?' Tony asked, frowning. 'Because if that's what it is, I promise the old man will deal with it.'

'I could deal with that myself, thank you,' Annys assured him. 'No, it's—look, you're probably going to find out anyway. Reid Bannerman is my ex-husband. We just don't get along any more, and it's going to be difficult enough for both of us without having to share a watch.'

After a moment of surprise, Tony said, 'You find someone willing to change with you, and I'll talk to Captain Walsh.'

Over breakfast, Jane agreed to take her place. The change-over wasn't even noticed by most of the others, Annys was sure. Tancred anyway was delighted to find her in the fourth mate's watch with him.

One of the tiny Japanese girls and Wendy, the middle-aged woman Annys had met the day before, made up

the female half of the team, with the tall German and
an American businessman who was a keen amateur photographer making up the male balance, the fourth mate
and another seaman giving the weight of experience.

Clean-up was the first item of the day's activity, and
when galley, cabins, saloon and the heads were all
sparkling and spotless the amateur crew rallied on deck
to learn about safety procedures, fire drill and what to
do if the call came to abandon ship. 'Although it's very
unlikely,' they were assured.

They learned some basics about the equipment on
board, then there were lessons in nautical knot-tying, in
managing anchor and sails, and after lunch they practised launching the ship's boats and rowing them.

Then came what they'd all been waiting for. 'One volunteer from each watch,' the captain said, 'to climb the
rigging.'

There was a moment's expectant silence. Then Annys,
sitting cross-legged on the deck with the rest of her watch,
saw a movement from Reid, leaning against the taffrail
at the stern, and she shot to her feet.

'Sure?' Tony asked her as she waited for him to tell
her what to do.

'Sure,' she replied firmly, ignoring Reid who was next
in line.

Tony checked their shoes first, making sure they were
all wearing sandshoes or trainers. Then they donned
safety harness and began the climb up the shrouds.

The ship swayed lightly on her anchors, and the ratlines gave under the climbers' weight, but Annys kept
her eyes on Tony climbing above her, carefully copying
his movements.

When they reached the yards, she scarcely had time to notice how far away the water was, following Tony's instructions to secure the clip on her safety harness before stepping on to the footrope. Then she was clinging to the yard, the rope under her feet moving as it took Reid's weight next to her.

They practised releasing the sail from the clews and gathering it up again, and once she had to snatch at the smooth, sun-warmed wood of the yard to keep her balance. Her heart gave a lurch of fright, and the blue-green water looked infinitely deep and dangerous, the safety rope terribly thin. The hardness of the deck so far below her didn't even bear thinking about.

Reid made a grab for her, letting the canvas slip from his hands.

'I'm all right,' she snapped, readjusting her feet. 'You take care of yourself!'

When they climbed down she could feel a line of fine sweat just under her hairline, but it was with a feeling of triumph that she leapt on to the teak boards of the deck. The fourth mate shook her hand before she turned to watch the others descend. Reid was already down, and as their eyes met he gave her an odd little smile, part congratulation, part challenge.

Once he'd said to her, 'You're the only woman I know who can keep up with me.'

She always had, and she certainly intended to now. He knew it, and the gauntlet had been picked up. Watching him stride away from her to take up his lounging position again at the stern, she felt an odd sense of excitement. If she'd known it, the light of battle was in her eyes.

* * *

By the end of the day more than half of the amateurs had tried the climb into the rigging. Some still held back, one or two swearing that they never would, others saying they needed time to psyche themselves up and make the attempt another day.

The Japanese girl on Annys's watch had gone up giggling and squealing but with every indication of enjoying herself hugely. Jane had made a competent, determined climb and returned grinning. Tancred had everyone laughing as he ostentatiously gathered his courage beforehand and humorously wiped his brow in thankfulness afterwards, muttering something about the things he did in the course of research. And Xianthe, who was on Reid's and Jane's watch, froze halfway up and had to be guided down by Tony.

'I feel a right twit,' she confessed to the other women in the cabin as they did their best to freshen themselves for dinner after a quick dip in the sea. 'You and Jane,' she said to Annys, 'made it look easy. Even little Miko and her friend managed it. But me...'

'I had an incentive,' Annys told her. And then, in case Xianthe asked what that was, added hastily, 'And Jane's done some mountain-climbing, haven't you, Jane?' She'd learned that the night before after dinner.

'Rock-climbing,' Jane corrected her. 'At Yosemite. It's different, though. At least there you've got a solid rockface in front of you most of the time. Don't worry, Xianthe, no one's going to force you up the rigging.'

At dinner Annys noted that people had altered their seating patterns, tending to gravitate towards their watch companions with whom they had spent the day. Xianthe had moved to the other table and was sitting beside Reid.

They seemed to be getting on well. Any man would be pleased to have Xianthe smiling at him the way she was, and Reid had never been averse to pretty women.

No use thinking about that, she admonished herself. It's all water under the bridge now, and Reid is free to have as many women as he wants.

She was free too, of course, and on that thought she turned a dazzling smile to Tancred who was asking her if she'd like something off the seafood platter he was holding.

On deck that evening someone brought out a guitar and everyone joined in a singalong. Annys sat with Miko and Tancred, who draped a casually friendly arm about each of their shoulders, and tried not to watch Xianthe and Reid, sitting in the shadows together. Xianthe had changed into a dress before dinner, a pretty, soft, flowered cotton affair with a low scooped neckline. Her dark, cloudy hair fell about her shoulders in loose curls and she looked utterly gorgeous and very feminine, the only woman on board not wearing shorts or trousers.

Determinedly, Annys dragged her gaze away, and concentrated on helping Tancred teach Miko the English words to a song. Next time she looked up Xianthe and Reid were gone. She didn't see them again until she was going down to bed. They were leaning side by side on the taffrail, and a slight breeze blew the woman's hair into Reid's face. She saw him lift his hand, heard him make a low-voiced, teasing comment, and Xianthe laughed, turning her head to him.

Annys set her teeth and went down the steep companionway so fast that she nearly fell.

*   *   *

The following morning they practised their new skills again, and after lunch the anchor was raised and the ship got under way, with just enough breeze to allow them to use the sails, helped by the still inept efforts of some of the amateurs who had eagerly climbed the rigging, and others pulling the ropes on deck.

Passing by some more of the two hundred islands of the bay, they gave a wide berth to the rocky outcrop of Cape Brett, where a tourist boat was motoring carefully through the hole-in-the-rock at Piercy Island. And then they were out of the harbour and sailing south within sight of the coast.

There was a flurry of excitement when a whale crossed the ship's path. Cameras and binoculars lined the ship's rail, and several people climbed the rigging just to get a better view of the magnificent creature, forging along obliviously, regularly spouting.

In late afternoon they anchored off The Poor Knights Islands, two larger island outcrops attended by a retinue of tiny islets and ragged stacks emerging from the sea. Clouds of seabirds hovered and wheeled over schools of small fish inshore, where the water was green with plankton. Gannets circled and then dived, wings held precisely, folding just as the birds entered the water like guided missiles.

'We can't land,' Tony said. 'We couldn't get a permit for so many people to go tramping round on the islands. But tomorrow you can swim and snorkel, we'll take parties in dinghies into one of the sea-caves, and those with experience—and the right gear—can do some diving.'

Annys looked at the thickness of the vegetation growing all along the clifftops, creamy cabbage-tree blossoms and the just bursting buds of crimson pohutukawa leavening the blanket of green. In Captain Cook's time there had been a Maori tribe living on Aorangi and Tawhiti-rahi, but now it was hard to imagine they had ever been inhabited. Of course, that was a long time ago, she reminded herself. The islands' people had been massacred in 1823 while their chief was away, and on his homecoming he had placed a tapu on them and sorrowfully left with the dozen or so survivors, never to return.

'Hey, is that a Poor Knights lily?' The amateur photographer was by her side, pointing at the cliff face.

'I don't know. Where?' Annys raised a hand over her eyes.

'Look, there. Maybe with a telephoto lens...' He began to rummage in the capacious camera pack slung on his shoulder.

Annys continued peering at the island, shading her eyes, until someone thrust a pair of binoculars into her hand. 'Take these,' Reid said. 'What are you looking at?'

Her first instinct had been to refuse Reid's offer, but that would have been childish, and embarrassing for the man beside her who was now screwing a long, bulky lens into his camera.

'It is,' she said, focusing the glasses on a sword-leaved plant with several large, spectacular scarlet heads of bottle-brush flowers, thrusting its way through the low-growing shrubs and leather-leaved matipo. 'Look.' She handed the glasses back to Reid. 'A Poor Knights lily.'

'They're rare, aren't they?' He lifted the binoculars to his eyes.

'Not here, but they were only discovered in the 1920s. There's a native broom too, that only grows here and on East Cape.'

He looked down at her as he lowered the binoculars. 'Taken up nature study, have you?'

'No, but I'm not illiterate,' Annys said tartly. 'I borrowed some books from the library before coming on this voyage.'

Beside them the photographer gave an exclamation of satisfaction and began snapping pictures.

Reid took Annys's arm and moved her further along with him. 'We're in this together,' he said very quietly, 'whether we like it or not. For the sake of the others on board, do you think we could make an effort to be civil to each other? It might help if you didn't read some insult into every word I say to you.'

'I'd really rather you didn't bother to say anything to me,' she said hotly.

'That's obvious,' he snapped. 'To everyone. It's creating an atmosphere already, and that's not fair to people who hoped to have a relaxing, enjoyable holiday.'

'Since when were you so sensitive about other people's feelings?' she scoffed.

'Is that fair, Annys?'

No, she supposed. He'd been particularly cavalier with her feelings, but that didn't make him a beast to everyone else. Particularly not to other women. She turned away from him, her lips tight.

'If I could,' Reid said, 'I'd leave the ship now——'

'That makes two of us,' she muttered.

'But I can't, and neither can you. So we're just going to have to put up with each other.' He paused. 'For what it's worth, I wasn't intending to be snide just now.'

'It just came out that way.'

'OK,' he said angrily. 'Maybe it did. I *apologise* for that.'

Apologising was something he didn't do often. The least she could do was meet him halfway. 'I'm sorry,' she said quickly, 'if I took it the wrong way. You're probably right. We ought to try to get along. It's only for a short while. I might manage it, if you can just keep out of my way as much as possible.'

'Right,' he said tightly. 'I'll try to do that.' He straightened and stepped back. 'Not easy on a ship this size, though.'

She smiled faintly in agreement. 'We should be able to manage it. Two minds with but a single thought...'

It wasn't the most tactful of quotations, she realised, her voice trailing off. She looked at him ruefully, biting her lip, and Reid laughed.

Her smile widened. They had always shared a sense of humour. Regret tugged painfully at her heart. Once laughter had allowed them to skate over many difficulties, but laughter hadn't been enough. And sex—lovemaking hadn't been enough. In the end the anger, the hurt, had been too much, and the laughter had died with their love.

Reid was looking down at her now with something in his eyes that made her heart momentarily stop, and killed the smile on her lips. His hand came up, and she flinched as he gently grazed her jaw with his closed fist.

She could feel the warm, fleeting touch on her skin for ages after he had silently turned away and gone along the deck out of sight.

*   *   *

There was a full moon that night, and nearly everyone lingered late on deck, admiring the silver patina on the calm, limitless water. The pohutukawa growing on the island made silhouetted patterns against a starry sky, and gannets still wheeled silently like ghosts, circling the masts. Even the breeze was warm.

When nearly everyone had finally given up and gone to bed, Annys remained sitting at the stern, along with the crew member on anchor watch, hypnotised by the night's beauty.

When she finally got up and grasped the shrouds, her foot on the rail, the sailor said, 'Going up?'

'Is it all right?'

'If you're careful. You've got your safety harness.'

'Yes.' She had it on over her sleeveless shirt, worn with shorts and rubber-soled shoes.

'Right,' he said. 'Enjoy yourself.'

She was sitting on the upper yard, one arm hooked about the mast, when she realised she had company. She wasn't sure when Reid had come silently up the ratlines, hadn't heard the snap of the clip on his safety harness. But he was settling on the other side of the mast, bare legs dangling from the yard. He'd pulled a dark T-shirt on over his swim briefs. In the moonlight she couldn't tell what colour it was.

Her skin prickled, but he had just as much right to sit here as she. And he didn't say anything, just acted as though she wasn't there. Which suited her, she told herself, turning away to contemplate the sea.

A ripple about fifty feet away caught her attention. She thought she saw a fin, then another ripple, then more. She caught her breath as something large and silvery leapt from the water, a streak of cold fire.

'Look!' she said, her voice hushed, and Reid said, 'Yes. I see him.'

Suddenly the sea was alive with a group of ten or twelve dolphins, streaking through the water, jumping, curving, the water flying off them like pieces of silver flame, sometimes two or three leaving the water at once, their gleaming bodies perfectly synchronised as they arced into the air and back into the sea.

And then they were gone, the water settling quietly as though they had never been there.

Annys let out a quiet sigh. She waited, hoping for their return, but knew that even if they came back it could only be an anticlimax to that first, unforgettable experience.

Reluctantly, she moved to climb down, finding Reid doing the same. They faced each other, both holding the mast, their hands inches from touching. He said quietly, 'That was a once-in-a-lifetime thing.'

'Yes,' she agreed. He was saying, Don't spoil it.

And she wouldn't. That would be like wantonly breaking something priceless. 'It was wonderful,' she said.

Reid nodded. 'Back to earth,' he said, indicating the deck below. 'You first?'

'Thanks.' She swung herself on to the ropes and began the descent.

CHAPTER FOUR

AFTER breakfast next morning the sea had an oily calm. Near the rocks it was clear as tap water. Sitting in rubber dinghies, they could see huge orange long-fingered starfish and purple anemones settled around tumbled rocks amid waving pink, brown and green seaweed.

They rowed under rock bridges and among standing outcrops decorated with clinging plants and washed by little waves, and then into an enormous cave with rough white walls.

Flippers and snorkels were brought out, and Annys and several others donned oxygen tanks and masks and dived into the limpid water. Soon she was swimming above a forest of kelp on the sea floor, swooping along a wide drift of sand studded with paper nautilus shells and blue starfish, watching crabs scuttle lazily into rock crevices, admiring a lacy orange rosette, then something golden and branched. Glittering fingerlings shot by in front of her mask, sparkling like jewels flung in the water, and she stopped warily to inspect from a safe distance a bloated orange and red fish with nasty spines.

Others divers waved at her, and, looking up, she could see the less experienced snorkellers near the surface. Someone touched her arm, and she turned to see Reid pointing out a long yellow moray speedily undulating away from them.

In that silent world their differences seemed far away. They explored underwater valleys filled with muted sun-

44

light, and soared like a couple of birds over hills forested
with hard coralline growths and soft, pale sponges
waving in the slight current. When they emerged from
the water and swam to their separate boats, Annys was
careful not to look in Reid's direction. The rapport they
had shared down there couldn't survive the real, everyday
world.

That night clouds covered the moon, a fresh breeze
swept the deck, and Annys went to bed early.

The swimmers who appeared for the morning dip were
noticeably fewer. There was a sharp, cold edge to the
air, and Annys and Jane were the only two among the
women brave enough to ignore it.

Some of the men were diving or jumping from the
ratlines, and Jane said, 'Let's try it. Can you dive?'

Annys was willing. They climbed as high as they dared,
higher than any of the men, and plunged down into the
freezing, limpid water. 'That'll show them,' Jane said
with satisfaction when they surfaced.

It would too, Annys agreed silently, smiling back at
her. Jane was a great believer in 'girls can do anything'.

Jane looked up and pursed her lips in a silent whistle.
'He's going to do it from there!'

Following her glance, Annys was just in time to see
Reid standing at the end of the lower yard, before he
launched himself outward and came down in a perfect
dive, arrowing into the water. The men cheered, and
Annys gradually forced her heart into a normal rhythm.
Reid was a good diver; he'd been senior champion in his
schooldays, he'd told her once in a rare moment of reminiscence. His head appeared, bursting from the water,
and he raised an arm to his admirers on deck.

'Beat that, girls!' someone called to them teasingly.

'Come on,' Jane said, her blood fired up. 'We can do it.'

Knowing it was a silly bit of bravado, Annys followed her back to the ship's side and up the ratlines, ignoring the men's encouraging whoops and whistles. They reached the lower yard, and Jane looked at Annys enquiringly, her hand on the shrouds that would take them higher.

Annys nodded, and Jane, already climbing, said, 'You don't have to, you know.'

'I know.' Annys was right behind her as they reached the upper yard, putting her bare feet on the foot rope. 'Let's go,' she said, inching along the yard.

She looked down when they were over the water, her stomach doing a slow revolution, and saw Reid's black head thrown back, heard him shout, 'Annys!'

She raised a hand and waved, then nodded at Jane and said, 'Let's go!'

They got their feet on the yard, poised momentarily, and launched themselves. The cold air rushed past her, then she was in the water, not as cleanly as Reid but it had been a creditable performance, she knew, even as the water took her deeper, deeper. It was a long way down.

She curved her body, reaching upward with her hands, saw the light above, Jane's shadow still beside her, and another shadow on the surface, hurtling towards them.

She came up gasping, and Reid flurried to a stop near by and said, sounding oddly furious, 'Are you all right?'

'Of course I am,' she said as soon as she'd got her breath. 'Why not?' She turned to Jane. 'You OK?'

The girl spat out some water. 'Yeah, sure.' She raised a triumphant fist to the watchers on deck, who were clapping now.

Reid glanced up. 'That was a hell of a high dive. Have you ever dived that far before?'

Jane said, 'No, actually. Probably won't again, either. It was fun though.'

Reid ignored her. 'Have you?' he asked Annys.

She squinted up at the yard. 'Probably not,' she said casually. 'It was great, though. Want to try it with me?'

For a second she thought he'd take her up on it. She recognised the look on his face as the one he got when presented with a challenge. Then he said, 'No. You've got goose-pimples. The water's bloody cold this morning.'

It was, but she stubbornly wouldn't admit she'd rather leave it, even after Jane had swum away from them and climbed the ladder to the ship.

Reid said as he watched the other girl climb on to the deck, 'Whose idea was it, anyway, that silly bit of showing off?'

'Jane's,' she told him. 'And talking of showing off, what were *you* doing?'

'I didn't do it for anyone's benefit but my own,' he said.

'Whose benefit do you think *I* did it for?' she demanded.

For once he seemed stuck for a come-back. She laughed and said, 'Don't flatter yourself, Reid. I gave up trying to impress you ages ago.' She dived under the water, coming up yards off, and swam away from him.

*   *   *

They hauled up the anchor again and continued the voyage. The captain made it known that he didn't approve of people diving from the yards, and no one attempted the feat again.

In the next few days everyone settled into the routine of the ship. Those who had been sick found their sealegs, and the amateur sailors became more competent, no longer looking blank when told to hoist the course or fasten the clews. Each watch, helped by the patient coaching of its regular crew members, forged itself into a more or less efficient team, and an element of friendly rivalry began to show itself. And as leaders emerged among the guest-crew members, the officers unobtrusively stepped into the background to keep a watching brief.

It was soon obvious to everyone on board that the two most competitive watches were the first mate's and the fourth's, and that Reid and Annys were providing the impetus. If one watch hoisted the full set of sails in eight minutes, the other did it in seven and a half. When one had all its members up the rigging in twenty seconds, the other achieved it in fifteen. When the wind died and they lowered the boats for races, Annys urged her watch to a victory won by inches, but in the tug-of-war on deck later Reid's team brought them sprawling to a laughing defeat.

If Miko's small size was sometimes a minus point for Annys and her watch, Xianthe was a handicap on Reid's. He had coaxed her up into the rigging by holding on to her most of the time, constantly assuring her that he wouldn't let her fall. After that she gamely took her place on the yards. With his support she joined in the various activities with gusto, and when they won the tug-of-war she cheered and threw her arms about his neck, receiving a laughing hug in return.

Of course it was all good fun; everyone treated the competition in a friendly spirit. Neither Reid nor Annys allowed their feelings to intrude on the pleasure of their shipmates. They didn't talk to each other, but in the general laughter and teasing one-upmanship between the watches Annys thought no one had noticed.

Their progress was leisurely, and late one afternoon they anchored offshore from another, uninhabited, beach and took to the boats for a barbecue meal on land. Fresh fish and rock lobster were on the menu, caught by the crew with the eager help of some guest voyagers. The crew also pointed out a freshwater stream with a deep water hole ideal for bathing, and the women spent a luxurious half-hour bathing and washing their hair before reluctantly allowing the men their turn.

'Real fresh water,' Xianthe murmured, sharing a bottle of shampoo with Jane and Annys. 'Oh, I hadn't realised how much I missed it!'

Annys wondered sometimes if Xianthe had known what she was getting into when she had booked the trip. It was obvious that she wasn't a particularly athletic person. She said she attended an aerobics class every week to keep in trim for her demanding career, but she seemed to regard it as a rigorous discipline rather than as something she did for pleasure.

Annys had to admire her determination. She never shirked, and seemed willing to try anything, even if she frequently made a mess of it. She would shrug off her failure with a rueful laugh and appeal for help to get it right.

She had a clear, true, though not powerful singing voice, and when they were all sitting round the dying fire after the barbecue it was Xianthe who led the singing. She was such a joy to listen to that once or twice the others let her carry on solo and applauded afterwards.

Annys looked across the fire at Reid, who was smiling as he clapped Xianthe's rendering of 'Summertime'. As she watched, he got up and went over to the other woman, his hand touching her shoulder in congratulation, their heads close as he bent over her raised face.

Annys got up and moved away from the fire, blindly heading along the cool sand in the darkness.

The voices of the others followed her, the sand gleaming pale, and the moonlight glimmered here and there on white waves shushing along the shore. She walked to the water and let it curl over her toes, the tiny bubbles hissing as it receded. The salty, clean smell of the sea mingled with the deep, rich scent of the bush that grew to the sand's edge. A rustling among the blackness of the trees made her swing round, startled.

'It's only me,' Tancred's voice said. 'That you, Annys?'

'Yes. I didn't know anyone else was out here.'

'Call of nature,' he explained, coming to join her at the water's edge. 'Lovely night, isn't it?'

'Lovely,' she agreed absently.

'Too good to waste?' he suggested tentatively, his hands going lightly to her shoulders. There had been an unaccustomed amount of liquor consumed tonight, not least by him. Usually the 'grog' was strictly rationed to a couple of glasses of wine or beer at dinner, but the captain had been lenient tonight.

Annys evaded him, laughing. 'Too lovely to waste skirmishing,' she told him. 'I came for a walk, not a moonlight snog.' Tancred was having a mid-life crisis, she had deduced. She gathered he'd always been something of a ladies' man. Now, with his youth rapidly slipping away, he went through the motions with most women he met, but his heart wasn't really in it.

'You're a hard, cold woman,' Tancred complained. He was swaying slightly as he spoke. Even in the moonlight she thought his eyes looked somewhat unfocused.

'Yes,' Annys agreed cheerfully. 'Come on,' she added, taking his arm to steady him. 'Let's go back.'

By the time they reached the circle round the fire he was leaning rather heavily on her shoulder, and she'd had to put an arm about his waist to keep him from stumbling. She was glad to relinquish her hold and let him sink to the sand, where he sat cross-legged and carefully straight-backed. Jane grinned at her, brows raised, and Annys sat down between her and Tancred and said quietly, 'I found him alone and palely loitering along the beach. I think he needed someone to point him in the right direction.'

Tancred must have heard part of it. He turned to Annys and said dramatically, 'Ah, *la belle dame sans merci*! You've broken my heart, you know.'

Annys laughed. Just as well he didn't have to swim back to the ship tonight. She looked across the lowering flame and saw Reid lounging along the sand in front of Xianthe. But he was looking at Annys, a disgusted expression on his face, mixed with anger.

He had no right, she thought confusedly, to look at her like that, anger of her own rising in response. She stared defiantly back at him, and when Tancred dropped a heavy arm across her shoulder again she let it lie there. There was no harm in him, and she wasn't going to create an unpleasant scene about a little over-amorousness just because Reid seemed to have taken it on himself to dis-approve. He was certainly in no position to be throwing stones.

Some people elected to stay ashore that night, dragging sleeping bags on to the sand. Annys was tempted, but, when she saw Reid preparing to stay, changed her mind and went back to the ship. To lie awake, hot and restless and wishing she had taken the chance of sleeping under the stars.

In the morning they tramped into the bush, the ground mushy under their feet with centuries of leaf-fall. Tiny creepers and intricate mosses grew alongside the barely discernible path, and they had to push back springy twigs laden with leaves to get through the close-growing trees. Huge ferns spread their silver-lined leaves over the trampers' heads. Of the trees that jostled each other, competing for the light, Annys recognised graceful weeping miro, and of course the giant kauri—enor-mously thick mottled grey trunks rising branchless, soaring above everything else until their crowns burst through the canopy to dominate the forest.

They came to a steep incline where a long gap in the trees ran like a broad, soft path of fallen leaves down to a shallow stream of water. Tony and the other mates exchanged grinning glances and finally Tony asked innocently, 'Anyone game for a nikau slide?'

The entire party instantly reverted to childhood. Somewhat bewildering the foreigners among them, everyone else hunted about the forest floor under the numerous nikau palms, and bore happily back several fallen palm branches with their distinctive thick, bowl-shaped ends where they had been shed from the trunks, just the right shape and size to sit in.

Grasping the tough dead stem in front of them, they took it in turns to career down the long slope, the trick being to get up a good speed but to stop in time to avoid being dunked in the stream at the bottom.

The Japanese girls and Xianthe descended shrieking and barely escaped that fate. Reid tumbled off his nikau near the end, rolling to the stream's lip, but saved himself and leapt up with fists held high, to ironic cheers from the onlookers. And Annys, following hot on his heels, managed to keep her balance while speeding down, and neatly brought herself to a halt by digging in her heels and pulling the stem round so that she slewed to a more or less graceful halt.

'Good going,' Reid said to her as she got to her feet and acknowledged the admiring applause from the others.

'Thanks.' She met his eyes with triumph in hers. Then Jane came rocketing out of control down the slope, slid between them, shouting, 'Way! *Aaargh*!' and landed with a forceful splash, showering them with water.

Together they bent to help her out, sodden and howling with mirth.

The crew had packed a picnic lunch which they ate at the foot of a formidable bluff of sheer grey rocks. Then an experienced climber among the staff took charge and gave them a brief lecture and demonstration, and invited those who wished to climb to the top of the bluff.

'Not me,' Xianthe said, shuddering. 'No way. There are limits, and I think I've reached mine.'

'There's a path to the top too,' Tony reassured her, 'if you'd rather do it the easy way. But if you've climbed the mast, this is a breeze, honestly.'

Reid and Annys stepped forward, and she was aware of a few knowing smiles among the others. It was decreed that Jane, as she had some experience, would work with the crew members who were spaced among the amateurs to help them if they got into difficulties. 'It's an easy climb, though,' Tony assured them.

'What we're doing,' the instructor told them, 'is free-climbing, using our bodies alone, hands and feet—and brains. We'll be using ropes for safety, but not as aids to pull us up, unless we're in trouble. The rock will help you.'

Annys saw Reid raise his brows in silent scepticism as he glanced at the formidable-looking grey wall before them, and she couldn't help smiling as he caught her eye before returning his gaze to the instructor.

'If you're stuck, relax and focus your mind. Concentrate on what's in front of you and on your next movement. If you're scared that's to your advantage. It'll stop you making stupid mistakes.'

There didn't seem to be any handholds or footholds on the smooth rock, but, as they began the ascent, and she watched the more experienced climbers above her and followed their movements, Annys discovered how a small crack could take a hand to haul her up, and a tiny irregularity in the rock give just enough purchase for her toes or the side of her foot, enough to get her to the next one.

When she seemed unable to find a foothold, Jane's voice said, 'Up a bit. You'll find a hold there, to your left.'

She found it and experienced a thrill of satisfaction.

'That's right. Now jam your toes in there to give you a grip while you find the next one.'

The rope secured about her midriff gave her a sense of security, but when she saw Reid, just below her and to one side, slide several feet down the face, she stopped, clamping her lips hard on a scream. Tony had him on a rope, and he came to a halt, flattened himself against the rock for a moment and then looked up, grinning, lifting a thumb.

Annys swallowed, and breathed again, and responded to Jane's 'Hey, you all right there, Annys?' with a shaky smile before resuming the ascent.

When they stood at the top, Reid coming over the lip soon after her, she saw that his hands were smeared with blood.

'What have you done?' she asked involuntarily.

'It's nothing. Scraped them when I slipped, that's all.' He looked at her with a sudden gleam in his eyes. 'Worried, were you?'

'Not particularly,' she said immediately. 'As they said, it's an easy climb, and with ropes. You weren't likely to come to any real harm.'

They were given a choice of walking down or abseiling. The crew rigged the gear, and one by one most of the amateurs were roped down the rock face. Even Xianthe took a deep breath and decided to try, landing at the bottom with obvious relief, but clearly pleased with herself as she waved at Reid and Annys peering over the top. Reid, waving back, said, 'She's a plucky kid, our Xianthe.'

When Tony asked, 'Who's next?' Reid turned to Annys and made a mock-courteous gesture, murmuring, 'Ladies first.'

'You can go,' she offered.

He shook his head. 'I insist.'

They were the only two left now. Wondering if his slip on the climb up had made Reid nervous, she looked at him consideringly and said, 'OK.'

But as she stepped towards the firmly anchored rope, Reid said to Tony, 'Actually, I thought I'd climb down.'

'Climb down?'

'Without the rope,' Reid added.

Annys whipped her head around.

The climbing instructor was grinning. 'Think you can make it?'

'Sure I can,' Reid said confidently.

'He's hurt his hands,' Annys heard herself say loudly. 'He can't!'

Tony was preparing to clip on her harness for the abseil, but she pushed it away. 'He can't!' she said again.

Reid was looking at her quizzically. 'Who says I can't?' he asked softly.

'Let's have a look at your hands,' the instructor said. 'Maybe you'd better not——'

'A couple of scratches,' Reid told him impatiently. 'It's nothing.'

Tony said, 'We can't accept responsibility——'

'My responsibility,' Reid told him. 'I'm not a teenager. If I wasn't sure I wouldn't do it.'

'I'll go first,' the instructor said.

Reid shrugged. 'As you like.' Turning to Annys, he said, 'On your way, then.'

'If you're climbing down, so am I,' she said.

'Don't be an idiot.'

'I'm no more an idiot than you are,' she argued. 'I haven't already had a fall and injured myself!' Her eyes narrowing, she said, 'That's what it's about, isn't it? It's because you didn't make a perfect climb, and now you want to prove something.' And also, she was sure, it was because he'd seen her wondering if the near-accident had shaken him.

'And if I do,' he said, 'is it any of your business?'

Tony and the other man were trying to look as though they weren't there.

'No,' Annys admitted finally. 'No more than my wanting to climb down is yours.'

His mouth tightened. Then he nodded grimly and turned to the instructor. 'Let's go, then.'

Tony looked at her determined expression and shrugged hopelessly. He murmured something about ropes, but Annys was already following the two men over the edge.

There was a murmur from below when it became obvious what they were going to do. Then everyone seemed to be holding their breath. In dead silence, except for an occasional quiet word of advice from the instructor, they inched their way down, moving feet and hands carefully, groping with their toes, their fingers, for every small purchase they could find.

'Use your feet,' the instructor reminded them. Then, 'Get your fingers into that crack there on your right, now twist them. Good, now feel with your foot, see if you can fit a toe in there—no, there. That's right.'

Once she paused, thinking there was no way she could get any further, that there was no place she could reach any more with her fingers, her toes.

Reid's voice said sharply, 'What's the matter, Annys? Are you all right?'

'Yes.' She took a couple of breaths, her cheek pressed against the hard stone. Concentrate on your next move, she remembered. The rock will help you...

Her toes touched something, slipped, swung. She gripped with her fingers on an inch-wide ledge above her. On the way up the instructor had said it was plenty big enough. On the way up they'd had ropes.

'To your right,' the instructor's voice came quietly. She moved her foot again, searching, and found a fissure, shoved her shoe into it, cautiously moved her hands, and was climbing down again.

When they finally leapt to the ground there was a rousing cheer, and Tony clapped them both on the shoulders. 'This goes into the ship's log as a record,' he said, before joining the others who were packing up ready to trek back to the ship.

Reid held out his hand to Annys, an odd light in his eyes, and she took it, feeling the rough, gritty palm, and the dampness of blood. When she drew hers away and looked at the pink smear on her own skin, he said, 'Sorry. I didn't think.'

'You didn't think much up there, either,' she said, suddenly swept by an inexplicable rage. Dropping her voice, she added, 'What the hell *were* you trying to prove, anyway?'

'What the hell were you?' he replied, and inclined his head questioningly at her, a sardonic curve on his mouth. Then he walked away without waiting for an answer.

CHAPTER FIVE

AFTER that landfall they cleared the coast for the open sea. There was nothing, Annys discovered, quite like the sensation of being on the yards when the ship was dipping and swaying on a sunlit sea with no land in sight. Fear was outweighed by the sheer pleasure of feeling the sea breeze and watching the gulls beating silently alongside, their ringed eyes on a level with hers. Sometimes on her off-watch she climbed up there just to experience it, and once stayed there for an hour.

When she came down, Reid was lounging against the rail at the bottom of the shrouds.

'Enjoy yourself?' he asked her.

'Yes. It's peaceful up there.'

He looked up, and then back at her. 'Good.'

She wouldn't have been surprised if he'd gone up himself and spent two hours aloft just to show her that he could.

A lot of Reid's time, Annys noticed, was spent helping Xianthe deal with tasks she found difficult, from rigging a block and tackle to stowing the sails. And she seemed to thrive on his attention. She'd gained confidence and was pulling her weight on the watch more effectively every day. 'This is great, isn't it?' she said, sitting on the deck housing with Annys and Jane while the wind cooled their faces and filled the white sails above them.

'Worth it all?' Annys asked.

59

'Worth being terrified out of your mind, and getting seasick, and going without showers and having to wash your hair in salt water?' Xianthe grinned. 'Just now, yes. This is how I imagined it. My great-great-grandmother was married to a whaling captain; she went on one of his whaling voyages with him. They used to take years. I read her diary when I was fifteen, and ever since I've had a hankering to experience a sailing ship for myself. It just makes me feel that I'm—sort of re-living her life.'

Jane said, 'Creepy!'

Xianthe laughed. 'No. But I reckon it'll make me a better actor. All this new stuff. And new people. I'm having so much fun. People have been awfully good about me being an absolute fool at knots and things.' Her eyes wandered, and Annys, following her gaze, saw that she was watching Reid walk along the deck to stand with one hand on the ropes, bracing himself against the rise and dip of the ship as it rode through the waves.

Maybe she ought to warn Xianthe that she might be riding for a fall. But of course she couldn't do anything of the sort. Xianthe was old enough to look out for herself, and a warning from an ex-wife would seem like nothing less than the revenge of a woman scorned. Or worse, simple jealousy.

And jealousy, of course, had nothing to do with it.

It was Xianthe herself who brought the subject up, the following day.

Dressed in a pair of shorts that showed off her long, tanned legs, and a skimpy tube top, she approached Annys where she'd been standing alone at the prow letting the wind blow her hair back off her face, and said quietly, 'Can I talk to you?'

'What about?' Annys tightened her hold on the rail, suspecting what was coming.

'Well...' Glancing at her and then away, to the rippling sea before them, Xianthe said, 'Reid. You used to be married, he said.'

'Used to be,' Annys agreed.

'I just wondered...' Xianthe's voice trailed off unhappily.

'You're not asking me for a character reference, are you?' Annys asked crisply. 'Because if so you've come to the wrong person.'

Xianthe looked shocked. 'Oh, no! No, it's just—well, I like him. I don't like very many men, as a matter of fact, and I just wondered...' she repeated. 'I mean, do you mind? Not that he's—nothing's happened between us. Only if he liked me too and if anything came of it— I wouldn't want to make you—you know— uncomfortable.'

'Why should you worry?' Annys asked.

'Because we're all on this ship together,' Xianthe pointed out.

'In the same boat,' Annys agreed drily. 'And it's not a very big one. You don't want to rock it, you mean?'

Xianthe nodded. 'Yes. You do see what I mean.'

'It's good of you to be so concerned,' Annys told her, 'but you needn't bother. Everything was over between Reid and me ages ago. Believe me, you're welcome to him.'

She turned and saw Reid standing by the companionway, staring towards them. Their eyes met for a moment, and she was surprised at the depth of hostility in his. Then he spun round and disappeared below decks.

The wind had freshened, and the captain headed for land, expecting what Tony called a 'willawaw'. In no time, it seemed, black clouds had raced up from the horizon to cover the sky, the blue sea had broken up in grey, choppy swells, and several people were hanging over the lee rail.

Volunteers were called for to lay aloft, and Annys found herself climbing the shrouds just behind Reid. The rain hit them as they reached the yards, and, while a dozen people fought to contain the sails and secure them, the ship bucked and shuddered and the wind tried to hurl them off their precarious footing on the ropes.

She scarcely registered that it was Reid working shoulder to shoulder with her until the task was done and some of the others were already climbing down. He looked at her with rain streaming down his face and plastering his hair to his forehead, and grinned and held out a hand, palm out.

Unthinkingly she grinned back, feeling the rain run into her mouth, her hair dripping, and slapped her hand against his in mutual congratulation.

He momentarily gripped it in his. 'OK?'

'OK!' Annys confirmed.

'Better get yourselves down!' Tony was shouting to them from the deck, and Reid looked down and waved a reassurance.

Annys shook back her soaked hair, her eyes still on Reid. She had a wild, fierce urge to stay where they were and enjoy the coming storm, and when he returned his gaze to hers she knew he felt it too, but she nodded and moved her feet along the rope to make the descent.

The squall harried them for several hours. Safety lines were rigged on the deck, and everyone who wasn't being sick was needed to work the ship. They were given rain-proof gear, but Annys was already wet underneath the bulky yellow parka. Walking near the rails, she got soaked in spray, and waves washed across the deck, filling her shoes with water and dragging at her ankles. Once the ship heeled broadside to the waves, the remaining sails flapping, and she lost her footing and went down, sliding feet first along sloping deckboards towards the churning sea.

A hard arm stopped her, pulling her back, and she grabbed for the safety rope, then turned to find Reid still with one arm clamped about her midriff.

'Thanks,' she said, raising her voice against the gusting of the wind and the hissing of the water. 'You can let go now.'

He looked down at her and suddenly bent his head, finding her cold lips with his.

The kiss was brief and hard, and his lips tasted of salt water and were cold, too, but as they parted hers she felt his warm breath enter her mouth, mingling with her own, and a quick, dizzy heat warmed her body.

Then he had moved away, and she stood up and struggled along the deck with him, holding the safety rope and forcing herself to concentrate on what Tony was asking them to do.

The captain started up the diesel engine, and the ship motored to Great Barrier Island, scurried into a bay and lowered anchors to ride the storm out. Annys went below to rub herself down and put on dry, warm clothes. On one of the bunks, Xianthe was clutching a stainless steel bucket in one arm, her face almost as pale as the cream-coloured pillow beneath her, her dark hair tangled. Her other hand pressed a dampened facecloth against her forehead, and her eyes were closed.

'Can I get you anything?' Annys asked as she did up her jeans and pulled on a thick woollen jersey.

Barely opening her mouth, Xianthe murmured, 'No, thanks.'

Annys dragged a brush through her hair. 'A drink of water?' she suggested. 'You don't want to get dehydrated.'

'No. Couldn't.'

Annys finished combing her hair and twisted a band around it before she said, 'If you can do without the bucket for a minute, I'll empty it for you.'

'I'll do it,' Xianthe said, trying to get up.

'Rot.' Annys took it from her. 'Back in a tick.'

'Thanks,' Xianthe murmured, and when she returned a few minutes later, 'Sorry, I ought to have——'

'No problem.' Annys looked at her thoughtfully. 'Most people feel better on deck, in the fresh air.'

'I know. I tried, but I just had to lie down. I feel like death.'

'I can see. We've anchored now. And the rain's easing. If you want to try again,' Annys offered, 'I'll help you. You'll need waterproofs; there are still some gusty showers about.'

Xianthe swallowed. 'I thought it wasn't jumping about quite so much. OK.'

Annys helped her up the companionway, and over to a narrow seat on the lee side where other unwell voyagers were sitting in various stages of recovery.

'How do you do it?' Xianthe asked Annys, sinking thankfully down as they made room for her. 'You look as healthy as a horse.'

'I'm lucky,' Annys said briefly. Several times today her stomach had felt decidedly queasy, but the wind and hard work had dispelled the incipient sickness. That and will-power, because no way was she going to allow herself the slightest weakness when Reid was around.

Think of the devil, she thought in the next instant. He had materialised beside her, and was smiling down at Xianthe. 'Not feeling too good?' he enquired sympathetically.

'That's the understatement of the year!' Xianthe told him weakly. But for the first time a faint colour came into her cheeks.

'I'll get you some water,' Annys promised her, moving quickly away. 'You don't have to drink it, but it might help.'

She took her time but when she got back Reid was still there, squatting on his haunches beside Xianthe. She was looking better by the minute, Annys thought. As she approached them, the ship gave a sudden shudder and heave, as a swell swept under the hull, and Annys staggered. Reid lunged forward, grabbing the glass of water with one hand and whipping it out of her fingers as he gripped her arm with the other.

'I'm OK,' she said briefly, and stepped back from him. 'I'll leave Xianthe in your tender care.' She smiled at the other woman and gave her a casual wave. 'See you.' Then she made her way carefully round to the other side and leaned on the rail, staring out at the misty rain and the bobbing, white-laced swells spitting little gobbets of foam.

Darkness was descending early, and on this side the wind was cold and still strong. No one else was in sight on deck.

She didn't hear Reid approaching until he said, 'Don't you think you're being a bit obvious?'

'What?'

As she turned her head he came alongside her, standing with his back to the rail so that he could see her face. He wore a yellow parka with no hood. Rain had darkened his hair even further, the short strands blown across his forehead by the wind. 'I said——'

'I heard. What exactly are you talking about?'

'You throwing Xianthe at me,' he said bluntly. 'What are you playing at, Annys?'

'Don't you like her? I thought——'

'Of course I *like* her,' he said impatiently. 'She's a nice girl and she's a trier. But I'm quite capable of making the running myself when I'm interested in another woman, thanks. I don't need your help. And I certainly don't need you to graciously make a gift of me, like a Christmas parcel.'

'I don't know what you're——'

'I heard you the other day. The wind was blowing from the bow. You women ought to be careful where you have your girlish heart-to-hearts.'

'I'm not sure what you heard, but——'

'"Everything was over between Reid and me ages ago,"' he quoted. '"You're welcome to him."' He paused, watching her. 'Is she?'

Annys shrugged. 'Sorry if we hurt your pride. I thought you'd be grateful.'

'I'm not,' he told her shortly. 'You haven't answered my question. *Is* she?'

She recalled vividly that kiss this afternoon, and looked away from him, afraid of what he might find in her eyes. 'I have no claims on you any more,' she reminded him distantly. 'Xianthe asked if I'd mind, and I said no.' Turning back to him, she added, 'And if you're not interested, it isn't fair to her to let her think that you are.'

His eyes narrowed as he gave her a penetrating look. 'And if I am?'

'Good luck,' she said crisply, and made to leave him. The wind caught at the hood of her parka and blew it off, leaving her face naked and cold.

Reid stepped in front of her, one hand on the rail barring her path. 'Good luck?' he echoed.

Keeping her expression carefully cool, Annys said, 'What else can I say?'

A calculating look came into his eyes. Equally coolly, he said, 'If you're going to wish me luck, you could do it properly.'

When they were married, she had always wished him luck with a kiss. One of the small rituals of married life.

'Don't be silly,' she said. 'That's hardly appropriate now. Besides—you said you didn't want to touch me again.'

'I already have, today,' he said. 'I find it's as addictive as ever. What about you?'

Oh, yes! Yes. But she wasn't about to admit that to him. She swallowed. 'Stop playing games with me, Reid. Go and talk to Xianthe.'

'Not until you wish me luck,' he said softly. 'Properly.'

She tried to push past him, her hands slipping on the wet, slick fabric of his parka. He hooked an arm about her and trapped her against the rail, looking down into her face. She caught her breath at the determination and naked desire she saw in his.

'Reid——'

'Annys,' he said, his face bending closer. 'Annys...'

And then they were kissing, mindlessly hungry for each other, as in the old days, his body against hers pinning her to the rail, her arms winding round his neck, clinging as her head tipped back to receive him, his hands retaining their grip on the rail to steady them against the motion of the ship.

Then he took one hand off the rail and placed it behind her head, sliding the loosened band from her damp hair, so that it flowed around them in the wind. He gathered the strands up in his fist and gently pulled, turning her head a little as his tongue dived into her open mouth, shifting his feet on the moving deck in an effort to get closer to her.

It was the frustration of their bulky wet-weather clothing that finally stopped them. He lifted his head and, still holding her hair, muttered, 'There isn't anywhere we can go on this damned boat.'

Staring back into his glittering eyes, Annys swallowed and said huskily, 'There isn't anywhere in the world for us, Reid. This is mad and you know it. We're not good for each other.'

She saw the quick flare of anger in his eyes. 'This was always good for us,' he reminded her, his hard body crowding her against the rail.

'There's more to marriage than this!' she insisted. 'And more to love.'

'Do you think I don't know that?' he asked roughly. 'What sort of callow idiot do you think I am?'

'I know just what you are,' she remembered, suddenly going cold. 'Let me go, Reid. I want to go below.'

He released her abruptly. 'I never thought you were one to run away, Annys,' he taunted her.

'I'm not running away.' She was retreating. There was a difference. 'Reid, we have to stop this now. We agreed before—it's the only way to survive this trip. Please.'

He looked at her sombrely. 'You feel the same way I do,' he said almost accusingly.

'All right!' she admitted, angry that he was pressing the point so insistently. Afraid of being drawn again into that world of delight and despair that had been her marriage to him. Because it couldn't last, and it had taken her all of the three years since the final break-up to recover even part of her former emotional independence. She couldn't face the thought of having to go through that grinding grief again. 'Old habits die hard,' she said, meeting his eyes defiantly. 'But they can be broken.'

'Is that what I am?' he asked. 'An old habit?'

'As I am with you,' she told him. 'That's all it is.'

He gave a harsh laugh. 'The hell it is,' he said. 'You are a fire in my blood, a flame on the horizon, a damned bleeding wound in my heart. No way are you anything as comfortable as a *habit*, darling!'

Annys felt her lips part, and quickly closed them. The words, the intensity of the bitter longing in his eyes, silenced her. She knew what he meant. 'We can't . . .' she said, her voice shaking. 'You know we can't make a life together. We tried——'

'Maybe we didn't try hard enough.'

'You mean *I* didn't.' Her head lifted.

'I didn't say that.'

'It's what you meant.'

The rain suddenly increased, hitting at them in great curtains, and the ship gave a lurch that sent them crashing into each other, coming up against the bulkhead.

'We can't talk here,' Reid said in her ear.

'What would be the use?' Annys cried despairingly. 'We've done all the talking, Reid. We have to put it behind us now, and get on with our separate lives. We can't call back the past.'

A hurrying wave splashed over the rail, and he staggered, then righted himself, staring down at her with his back to the elements, sheltering her from them. 'I won't plead with you,' he said. 'But I haven't finished with you yet, Annys.'

She blinked rain from her eyes. 'You're not threatening me, are you?'

'I'm telling you. If you want to regard it as a threat, that's your privilege.' But he looked dangerous, standing there with the storm clouds behind him, his mouth stubborn, and a frown on his brow.

From the companionway the brassy note of the dinner bell pealed. An ironic cheer from the hardy mingled with a few theatrical groans from the seasick.

The faint grin that Reid mustered at that eased the tension. 'Shall we go and eat?' he suggested.

The morning dawned limpidly with a pale sunrise. The rain had gone, and the ship rocked on a glassy sea broken only by the gentlest ripples.

Captain Walsh, taking pity on his lubberly crew of amateurs, decreed a day ashore.

Last night Annys had lain on her bunk renewing her original plans to leave the ship and cut short her voyage. But it would make her very conspicuous, Reid would know perfectly well why she was leaving, and she hadn't even had the forethought to pretend seasickness as an excuse. Besides, she was hooked now on tall-ship sailing, enjoying the sea, the wind in the sails and in her hair, and getting a great deal of pleasure out of learning to work the ship. Why should she allow Reid's presence to spoil it for her? And wouldn't he regard her departure as some kind of victory, as though she had turned tail and run from him?

Xianthe and one or two of the others who had been among the worst sufferers preferred to recuperate by lying about on the shore, but for the adventurous there was a hike into the hills through heavy bush to the site of an old kauri dam.

The dam, once used to store cut timber before being opened to wash the logs downstream to the harbour, was still partly intact. After admiring the early bushmen's workmanship, the trampers launched inflatable canoes, which they had hauled along with them, on the stream below, and had a hilarious and somewhat damp time negotiating the rocks and narrows. Racing, Annys and Jane tipped their craft and got dunked, but righted it in time to finish neck and neck with Reid and one of the other men, who had got theirs jammed between two smooth boulders.

On their return they were told that the captain proposed a night's sailing down to the Coromandel Peninsula. Even Xianthe, having had the day to recover, greeted the idea with enthusiasm. They left the rugged island when sunset was overlaying the water with a wash of gold, and accomplished the short voyage by moonlight. Nearly everyone was on deck for at least part of the night, entranced by the ghostly white sails carrying them almost silently on a black, glinting sea.

By dawn they were anchored off Hot Water Beach, and after the usual cold morning dip in the sea some of them swam to shore to make themselves holes in the sand and luxuriate in the warm water that bubbled up from hot springs deep in the earth. 'If you dig down very far,' Tony warned them, 'the water will be too hot. Make your bath shallow, or dig it where the waves can wash in and cool it.'

'Ah, bliss!' Tancred said, easing himself into a long hollow next to Annys. 'After that disgusting overactivity yesterday, this is just what I need.'

'Why did you come yesterday?' she asked him. She'd half expected him to spend the day resting.

He gave her a deliberately lecherous leer. 'Why, the better to be near you, my dear!' he purred, wolf-like.

Annys laughed. 'You're impossible, Tancred!'

'You don't believe me?' He levered himself up and leaned his elbows on the strip of sand between them, smiling as his eyes travelled over her scantily covered body from neck to toes. 'Have you any idea how delectable you look right now?'

Annys scooped up some warm water and threw it at him. 'Behave yourself, Tancred!' she admonished him.

Tancred grinned, then leaned over and audaciously planted a kiss on her lips. 'Never refuse a dare,' he said smugly, settling back into his own private pool.

Annys shook her head in warning, but her lips curved wryly. He was irrepressible. Turning away from him, still smiling, she intercepted a grim look from Reid, a few yards off.

Defiantly, she held his contemptuous gaze for a moment or two, then let her head fall back on the sand, her eyes closing. She wouldn't think about Reid. She wouldn't think about anything.

The insistent boom and whisper of the waves, the burgeoning sun on her face, the warmth of the water on her limbs lulled her almost to sleep. Distantly she heard voices now and then, but she shut them out of her consciousness, until the one that still had the power to rouse her said, 'Are you intending to stay here all day?'

Reluctantly opening her eyes, she found Reid staring down at her. His long legs and his chest gleamed with droplets of water, and the wind ruffled his hair.

'The others went back long ago,' he told her. 'We've missed breakfast, and the tide's coming in.'

Even as he said it, a wave came racing up the beach and swamped her warm bath with a shock of unwelcome cold.

Annys yelped and sat up.

Laughing, Reid extended his hand to her and she instinctively grasped at it, hauling herself up.

The wave receded about their feet, and she staggered. Reid let go her hand and grasped her shoulder to steady her. It brought her very close to him, and she felt his grip tighten, then his other hand came up to hold her there.

She raised her eyes to his and saw the heavy-lidded look of desire on his face, and whispered, scarcely breathing, 'No.'

Anger lit his eyes now. 'You let that middle-aged roué kiss you, and apparently you enjoyed it—why not me?'

Her own anger rose to match his. He had no right to question her actions, no right to his evident, and needless, jealousy. Rashly, she said, 'Perhaps because I know I *wouldn't* enjoy it!'

'You liar!' he said softly, and inevitably his mouth came down on hers, even as she tried to turn her head away.

Her hands slipped on his bare, wet skin, and he wrapped an arm about her, trapping hers and reminding her of how little she was wearing, unlike the last time when the heavy waterproofs had impeded them. A slow heat unravelled inside her as his mouth insistently explored hers in a knowing kiss, forcing her lips to part for him, tracing the outline of them with his tongue, then gently nipping them with his teeth, nudging her mouth wide under his, so that her head fell back against his cradling hand and her body arched into the curve of his. Her breathing quickened and the blood sang in her veins.

A wave slapping around her ankles brought her back to some semblance of sanity. She doubled her fists and pushed against him, tried to kick at him with her bare feet, and with an effort tore her mouth away from his.

He still held her, his eyes glittery as he looked down at her flushed face. 'Tell me you didn't enjoy that!' he muttered, his voice thick.

She longed to hit him. It would have given her the greatest satisfaction to rock him clean off his feet. And it probably would give *him* a good deal of satisfaction to know that he had rattled her that much. She swallowed and said grittily, 'You must be losing your touch, Reid, if you have to resort to force to make a woman kiss you!'

Surprisingly, a tide of colour darkened his tanned skin. 'Only with you,' he taunted. 'But it wasn't always like that, was it, Annys?'

She wished he would stop reminding her of the past. That was something she didn't want to think about. She would never have thought, in those days when the slightest invitation would send her flying willingly into his arms, that they could ever come to this bitter confrontation. She swung away from him and went striding down the beach, running the last few yards, afraid that he would catch up and see the tears foolishly chasing each other down her cheeks before she reached the concealing safety of the water.

CHAPTER SIX

REID had said to her once, as they had lain on a bed on the third day of their Hawaiian honeymoon, their bodies damp with afternoon heat and the aftermath of their lovemaking, 'I want you all the time. You will tell me if I'm asking too much of you? Don't let me tire you out.'

'I want you too,' she had said, drowsily tracing patterns with a fingernail on his bare chest, then laying her cheek against it, listening to his heartbeat. 'I'll tire you out first,' she promised, peeking up at him with teasing eyes.

His chest shook with silent laughter. 'Is that a challenge?'

Annys sat up, smiling down into his eyes. 'If you like. Men don't have as much stamina as women.'

'Is that so?' His eyes dropped to her bare breasts, and he lifted a hand, lazily circling a pink aureole with one finger. 'You wanna bet?' he enquired softly, his eyes darkening as he watched the effect of that careless caress.

Annys tipped her head back and closed her eyes, the better to enjoy the slow, tingling return of desire. 'Mmm.'

'Anyway,' he said quietly, turning his attention to her other breast but still lying with one hand casually tucked under his head, 'how would you know? You've never slept with any man but me.'

She opened her eyes and looked at him, her mouth curving in a smile. 'I read a lot,' she said succinctly. 'And you needn't look so smug.'

'I feel smug. No, I feel pleased and proud and humbly surprised.'

'Humbly?' Annys cocked her head at him. Humble wasn't a word that she'd thought would be in Reid's vocabulary.

As if the admission might have embarrassed him, he lifted his head to free his hand, and said huskily, 'Stop talking, woman, and come here.'

And he drew her down to him and stopped her mouth with his.

That had been one of the best times of all. Already sated, but with the mutual, teasing challenge to spur them on, the initial sluggishness of returning passion allowed long minutes of tender stroking, of lazy, intimate explorations and soft, sweet kisses. The gradually building delight was accompanied by low laughter and quiet, nearly motionless embraces that lasted for minutes at a time, when they almost drowsed before a caressing hand, a wandering mouth, sparked a shudder of pleasure or a murmur of encouragement.

Accustomed to explosions of shared need, they found this time a new dimension to their lovemaking, and when she received him into her body they paused by tacit consent to gaze at each other with awe and ecstasy, not wanting to leave the exalted plane that they had reached, even for the final release of their mutual joy in each other. For a long time they stayed together, breathing carefully, smiling now and then, touching each other's faces, exchanging quick, almost furtive kisses. Until, unable to postpone it any further, Annys drew his head down to hers and closed her eyes and opened her mouth to him, and felt him move gently, then more and more urgently, and finally she was flying, flying, breaking up into shining, bright pieces of pleasure, flinging back her head because she had to give voice to it, as Reid gave voice to his with his mouth against the warm skin of her throat.

It was a long, long time before they came back to earth, and stirred against each other, and nuzzled contentedly, and Annys settled her cheek on Reid's shoulder and slept.

Later they got dressed and went out for a leisurely dinner, eating without tasting, drinking an expensive wine that Reid had ordered, and finishing the bottle without noticing. Every time they looked at each other, Annys felt her heart pound with love for him, with wanting him again. And she knew that what was in her eyes was what she saw in his, so that after a while she was afraid to look at him at all. Afraid that everyone else in the restaurant would know, that the very air between them would be scorched.

When he put a hand over hers and asked, 'Do you want dessert? Or coffee?' she couldn't even speak, just shook her head.

He stroked her hand, his fingers strong and lean over hers. 'What do you want, then?' he asked.

Annys looked up at him. 'You,' she said baldly.

Reid took a quick breath. 'Thank heaven,' he breathed. 'I don't think I can stand another five minutes without having you.'

They never even made it back to the hotel. They'd been staying at a beach holiday resort, walking the half-mile or so to the restaurant along a white road.

When Reid said, 'We could go back via the beach,' Annys nodded agreement. They took off their shoes and held them as they walked, arms about each other. It was late and there was no one about. The moon kept disappearing behind dark, ragged clouds. Their feet tangled in a drift of dried seaweed, and as they paused to extricate themselves Reid dropped a quick kiss on her mouth before they walked on. Then he stopped her for another, longer kiss, his fingers kneading the smooth skin of her waist beneath her thin silk dress.

They came to a huge, bleached driftwood log and he kissed her again, deeply, while she held him with her arms flung about his neck, her shoes forgotten on the sand.

He moved his arms from her waist, stroked his hands downward and then gripped her hips, lifting her to stand on the log, her bare feet on the cool, weathered wood. His hands were under her skirt, smoothing her thighs, his head tipped back as she bent over him, giving him her mouth.

'Undo your dress,' he said against her lips, still touching her, and she opened the tiny buttons down the front of the low-necked, fitting bodice, glad that, because straps tended to show, she hadn't worn a bra tonight. She pushed aside the fabric, revelling in the sound of Reid's indrawn breath as he looked at her.

She put her hands in his hair and drew him to her, uttering a soft cry at the first warm, eager touch of his mouth, her knees sagging a little as she swayed closer

to him, feeling his firm hands shaping her body under
the concealing skirt of her dress.

After a while he lifted her down, holding her to him,
and said, 'I can't wait, darling. I want you now, here.
All right?'

'All right,' she agreed, covering his face with tiny,
urgent kisses. 'I don't want to wait, either.'

He shrugged off his shirt and made a pillow for her
head of it, and spread the skirt of her dress on the sand,
and in the shadow of the driftwood they lay down and
pleasured each other once more.

Afterwards they dusted sand off each other, and Reid
did up her dress for her, fumbling at the buttons. He
didn't bother to put on his shirt, slinging it carelessly
across one shoulder, his other arm hooked about her
waist. He brushed his lips across her temple. 'I love you.
You're the most incredible girl I've ever met. I love to
make love to you.'

She wasn't the first for him. Annys had known that,
of course. She felt a twinge of jealousy, quickly stifled.
He was older than her, and men even nowadays were
expected to show off their sexual prowess, to test their
manhood while still in their teens. But he'd not married
before, never asked any of those other girls—and she
had no idea how many that was, hadn't enquired—to
be his wife.

And the fact that he was no novice at lovemaking
didn't mean he'd been in the habit of sleeping around.
She was sure he wasn't the type to do that. He'd obviously been attracted to her when they'd met, but he'd
never made her feel the way some men did when they
covertly or frankly ran their eyes over her as though she

were on sale. And he didn't spend half his time when they were together watching other women, either, although Annys had noticed the interested glances many of them couldn't help casting at him. He was too good-looking not to attract some feminine stares, but he gave no sign of noticing them. In fact, from the moment he'd first set eyes on Annys, he'd given her the heady impression that he never wanted to look at anyone else.

She had been equally smitten. From the night they'd met there'd been no one else for either of them.

It had been in a ski hut on Ruapehu, where she was a weekend guest of married friends who belonged to the club that owned it. In the party of ten people there was a man who she knew had been invited along for her benefit. He was nice, and she'd been getting on well with him that day on the slopes, and was happy to sit beside him as they sat about a roaring fire in the evening swapping stories of mishaps and good runs, and singing.

Then someone had come banging on the door, and three men came in dusting snow off their clothes and explaining how they'd taken a wrong turning on the mountain, it was snowing heavily and they couldn't make it back to their own hut.

Of course they were made welcome for the night, and they accepted hot drinks and everyone shifted about to make room for them round the fire because they had just come out of the snow and must be cold.

Introductions were made and the tallest of the three stopped by Annys and smiled at her as she began to shuffle along the wooden seat she was on. 'Don't move,' he said, 'I can sit in front of you, if it won't block the warmth from you too much.'

She looked up into dark eyes with flecks of green in them in a tanned face, saw the quick flare of interest and felt an answering flicker of warmth and excitement. 'It's OK,' she said. 'I was getting a bit too hot, anyway.'

He stood for a moment smiling at her, and then turned and sank down with his back to her, his arms resting on raised knees.

She looked at the dark head in front of her, the dark hair with a hint of wave combed back but a little ruffled, and the hand that hung casually across his other arm. A strong hand, capable, long-fingered and broad-palmed, with short, clean nails. Not the hand of a manual worker but very masculine all the same.

He turned his head and found her watching him, and smiled again.

For an excuse, she said, 'I didn't catch your name.'

'Reid,' he said. 'I'm Reid Bannerman. And you're Annys.'

He said it as though her name was special, looking into her eyes.

She said, 'You've a good memory.' She'd only had three new names to learn; he'd just been introduced to ten people.

'Not particularly,' he said.

She'd looked away then, because his eyes told her she knew why he'd remembered her name, and she wasn't quite ready to admit it to him. Never before had she been so strongly, instantly attracted to a man. She found it unsettling, a bit scary.

Perhaps he realised it, because after a thoughtful moment he began talking to the man beside her in a casually friendly way, and when he next spoke to Annys it was in the same tone, a simple query about how she'd found the mountain, and how often did she ski?

From then on it was easy. Annys managed some equally casual replies, telling him she couldn't ski as often as she would have liked, but letting him know she was fairly competent. She found out that he was a consulting engineer and had worked all over the world.

'Consulting on what?' she asked.

'Buildings, bridges,' he answered, 'roads sometimes, oil rigs once or twice. I specialise in advising on earthquake resistance. Just recently I've been helping plan the rebuilding of a town in Japan that was hit last year. What do you do?'

'Nothing so exciting.' After leaving university with an arts degree she'd taken a course in design, but jobs were hard to get, and she'd worked in a fashion boutique for six months, then in a sports goods store. Now she was a part-time instructor in a gymnasium, giving her time to design and make sportswear which she was beginning to sell to retailers. 'I'm just starting out in my own sportswear business,' she told him. 'But I don't know yet if I'm going to make it.'

'You'll make it,' he predicted.

He couldn't possibly know, of course, he'd only just met her, but the quiet certainty in his voice was an ego boost.

'You have that look about you,' he told her, 'that says, "I can do anything".'

It was a look and an attitude that she had worked at. Some men were repelled by it, preferring women who could make them feel strong and needed. This man looked as though he found it interesting, even attractive. His eyes held approval, and a hint of challenge, as though he would have said, Go on, then, show me! Show the world.

She would too, she thought, returning the look unwaveringly. Something about him put her on her mettle. She'd never cared what anyone thought of her, had forged ahead in her own way for her own satisfaction without worrying about other people's opinions. But she wanted Reid Bannerman to know that she was someone, that she was a success.

When the other man, the one with whom she'd spent an enjoyable day, yawned and said, 'I'm off to bed,' she glanced at the clock and saw how late it was. Some of the others had already gone off to their bunks. As he made for the ablutions room, she got up in her turn. Reid Bannerman caught at her wrist and stood too, holding her in a light, firm clasp. 'Are you two a couple?' he asked her, glancing towards the man whose name she could scarcely recall now.

Annys shook her head. 'I only met him this weekend.'

He said, 'You only met me tonight.'

There was no answer to that. Already he was important to her, in some tentative but definite way.

'Come skiing with me tomorrow?' Reid said abruptly.

'Yes,' Annys said. Of course she would. There was no question of turning him down. Whatever was between them demanded that they spend some time together, discover each other, find out what it was that had forged an instant bond between them, as though in some strange way they'd recognised each other.

He said, 'Good,' and let go her hand. For a moment longer they stood close together, facing each other. Then Annys turned away and left him.

* * *

The run he suggested in the morning was one of the advanced slopes and she hadn't tried it before. When she told him that in answer to his query, he said immediately, 'We'll take another one instead.'

'No.' She set her jaw stubbornly and said, 'I've enough experience to tackle it. I've not had anyone to ski it with. I want to do it,' she insisted, as she saw he was about to argue. 'If you won't come with me, I'll ski it by myself.'

She knew it was going to be a test of her skill, but today, in his company, she knew too that she could indeed do anything.

And she was proved right. They pushed off together at the highest point they were able to get to, and swooped down shoulder to shoulder, the wind whooshing by them, their skis hissing over the deep, smooth powder, leaving twin tracks behind them on the steep slope.

Annys swerved to avoid a snow-covered hump; Reid went right over it, soared briefly and landed perfectly balanced and went speeding on, his poles free in his hands. Behind him, Annys laughed and made an effort to increase her speed, swooping past him a little further down. She knew she was going so fast that she was barely in control, but she'd told Reid she could do this, and she was determined she was going to do it well.

Then he was beside her again, smiling at her, and she risked a brief smile back before returning her concentration to keeping her balance and watching for obstacles.

First she and then Reid would fly ahead, but the other would pole after the leader and catch up. When they finally reached the bottom side by side and in a flurry of snow brought themselves to a controlled halt, she turned to Reid, panting and laughing, her eyes bright with exhilaration. 'That was terrific!'

He looked down at her, grinning as he pulled off his snow goggles. 'You're pretty good,' he said with respect. 'I thought I'd have to hold back for you.'

Annys said almost fiercely, 'Don't you ever hold back for me!'

He regarded her with concentration for a moment and then said, 'Right. I won't.'

From the first she'd known that was one of the things he liked about her, that she never asked for special concessions, and was always able to match him.

At the end of the day he fished a card from his pocket and gave it to her. It had 'Bannerman International' written on it in bold black type, and underneath, 'Engineering Consultants' and Reid's name.

'Consultants?' she queried. 'In plural?'

'I've more work than I can handle.'

'How many in the firm?'

'Three engineers, a couple of trainee-assistants, a sec-retary, a telephonist.'

He asked for her address and telephone number and she gave it without hesitation. He wrote it down in a small green-covered pocket diary, looked at it and said, 'I'm based in Wellington at the moment. But I'll come to Auckland as soon as I can manage it, spend a few days. I'll be in touch.'

She didn't question that he would. Even when two weeks went by and she hadn't heard from him, she knew it would happen.

One afternoon she'd just got back from the gym and was making a cup of coffee before settling down to her drawings, when the phone rang.

'Reid,' he said in answer to her casual hello. 'Reid Bannerman. Remember?'

Of course she remembered. She realised she'd been counting the days.

He took her to a restaurant for dinner, then to a nightclub, and they danced, sometimes apart and sometimes close, and drank a little and listened to the music, talked in snatches when the music let them, and danced some more. Then he took her home and said, 'Can I come in?'

And Annys, knowing what he meant and suddenly nervous, said, 'No. Not yet.' Then bit her lip because that was giving away more than she'd meant to.

He laughed quietly, and said, 'May I kiss you goodnight?'

Silently she lifted her face, and he took it tenderly between his hands and kissed her very, very gently. And left.

Annys let herself into the old house that she shared with two other girls and the fiancé of one of them, and shut the door, feeling almost sick with disappointment.

He had not made even the slightest suggestion of seeing her again. Was he one of those men who demanded instant gratification, and, if they didn't get it, went off to greener fields?

If so, he wasn't worth bothering with, she assured herself. And took herself to bed feeling thoroughly depressed, tempted to cry herself to sleep.

All that changed the following day when he phoned as she was getting ready to go to the gym. 'What are you doing today?'

'I'm working until two,' she told him.

'I have a meeting at one. I should be through by two-thirty. Do you surf?'

'Yes, I have a board.'

'Good. I can pick you up at three. Your place?'

It didn't occur to her then that he was taking a lot for granted. She said, fine, that would suit her perfectly, and when he'd said goodbye hung up with a smile on her lips and a singing heart.

It had kept on singing as they rode the waves at Piha on a wild, cool summer's day when the water thundered on to the black-streaked sand as though determined to pummel it into submission. Growing tired of fighting the rollers, they climbed Lion Rock and stood on the summit, buffeted by the wind and looking down at the curling breakers trying to scramble up its face, and held hands on the way down. Then they went into the water without the boards, bodysurfing in on the thundering waves again and again, and coming out breathless and cold, their skin stinging with the salty force of the ocean.

When they reached home her flatmates were back from work and she invited Reid to stay for a meal. He left quite early, drawing her out to the old front porch with him, closing the door behind them, and this time he didn't ask if he could kiss her. He pulled her into his arms and brought his mouth down on hers as if he knew that she'd been waiting all day for this, and as if he had too.

'I have to go away again,' he said when they had drawn apart a little, her hands held in his warm clasp.

'When?'

He sighed, frowning down at her fingers in his. 'Tomorrow.'

I'll die! Annys thought. She clutched at his hands and then, ashamed of herself, tried to free them, but he wouldn't let her.

'Three weeks,' he said, answering the question she hadn't asked. 'I've got a job on in the Cook Islands. I have to go, Annys.'

'Of course you do.' Of course he couldn't rearrange his life, his work, for her.

'I'll see you when I come back,' he told her. 'Promise.'

Annys nodded. He seemed to want something more, and she said, 'I'd like that.'

Reid smiled then. 'I can't wait. You wouldn't...' He paused, then dropped her hands and said, 'No.'

'What?'

He shook his head. 'Never mind.'

'You can't go off for three weeks and leave me wondering what on earth it was you were going to say,' Annys complained.

He smiled wryly. 'I was going to say, you wouldn't think of getting a place on your own while I'm away, would you? Much as I like your friends, your flat's short on privacy.'

Tempted, Annys hesitated a moment before common sense intervened. 'You're right,' she said. 'I wouldn't. For one thing, I can't afford to,' she added frankly.

'And you wouldn't let me help, of course,' he guessed.

'I certainly wouldn't!'

'Not that sort of girl, Annys?'

'Did you think I was?' she asked him, slightly shocked.

Reid shook his head. 'Not for a minute. I'm not that kind of guy, either. I don't make a habit of offering to pay the rent for a woman. It wasn't a love-nest I was thinking of.'

It crossed her mind that, for all she knew, he had one already, or several. He travelled a good deal, and maybe it would suit him to have a few cosy establishments in his different ports of call.

'What are you thinking?' he asked her. 'That's a very odd look you're giving me.'

Embarrassed, she said, 'I was thinking I don't know very much about you.'

'Ask.'

'Do you have a family?'

'Sort of. A brother in America. A sister in Perth. I see them occasionally when my work takes me near. Both my parents are dead. They were divorced when I was ten. I stayed with my father, but my younger brother and sister went to live with my mother. Eighteen months later she committed suicide.'

'How awful,' Annys said. 'I'm sorry.'

'It was hard for my brother and sister. Harder still for my father. He blamed himself, and it haunted him for the rest of his life. Dad died of lung cancer two years back. What about your family?'

'My parents married late and I was their only child. They live in Northland, have done all their lives.'

'They must have missed you when you left home.'

'I suppose, but they wanted me to do well, to go to university. I had to come to Auckland for that.'

'And stayed.'

'Northland has one of the highest rates of unemployment in the country. I had no hope of getting work there.'

Still holding her hand, he brushed a strand of hair from her face, his fingers lingering on her cheek, shaping the curve of her ear, caressing the line of her neck. When they wandered to her neckline, she moved slightly, and his hand fell away from her.

'You're a bit wary of me, aren't you?'

Annys shook her head. 'Of course not! Should I be?'

'Not for any reason I can think of,' he assured her seriously. 'Can I ask you to show me you're not?'

He didn't need to explain. She put her hands on his shoulders and placed her lips warmly on his. Felt his arms go round her, and then her back was against the wall by the door and his hands touched her breasts through the soft cloth of her sweatshirt. Her mouth clung to his, the taste and scent of him filling her with a wild, desperate longing. One hand clutched a handful of his shirt as though it would steady her, and the other touched his hair, his face, blindly.

Knowing what she wanted, he shifted his feet and bent her body to his, his hands sliding round to her waist and down, holding her as he went on kissing her.

Annys made a little sound in her throat, and he lifted his head and whispered, 'What is it, sweet? Darling?'

'I . . . n-nothing.' Her teeth were chattering. She was overwhelmed by sensations that she had never experienced so powerfully before. She felt as though she'd left the ground behind and was floating somewhere among the stars. The strength of her feeling for this man was almost frightening.

She pushed against him, tentatively, and he eased his hold on her, his lips nuzzling her brow. 'Annys,' he said, quietly triumphant, 'I do believe you want me almost as much as I want you!'

'Probably more,' she confessed with stark honesty, and he laughed delightedly, breaking the tension.

'Impossible,' he told her, holding her hands tightly in his. 'I suppose you wouldn't consider coming back to my hotel with me?'

With an effort, Annys shook her head.

'No,' he said wryly. 'I thought not. And you're right. You deserve better.' He smiled down at her. 'I won't rush you, Annys.'

He'd kissed her quickly then and was gone, leaving her feeling a mixture of regret and relief, shock at herself, and doubt.

He never wrote when he was away, either before or after they were married. He'd phone her, say, 'I just wanted to hear your voice. How are you? What have you been doing?' And he'd talk about the job, the place where he was, the people he worked with. Mostly they were men; she always pictured him among men, poring over plans and blueprints, climbing half-finished structures in hard hats, talking over boardroom tables. Strange, she thought, years later, that with all her own staunchly held ideals of feminism, her belief that men and women were equally capable of doing almost any job in the world, she had imagined Reid's world as a totally male one. Strange and in hindsight rather stupid. Perhaps, subconsciously she'd been wilfully blinding herself.

Those three weeks before he came back she seemed to live in a hiatus, a world where nothing was quite real, where she functioned like a robot, insulated from everything about her by a kind of warm shell where she lived alone and waiting.

And then he was there again, lounging outside the gym when she finished work, and without thought she flew into his arms and they kissed as if they'd been parted for years.

They had the rest of that day, which they spent picnicking in a park overlooking the harbour, and talking— agreeing and disagreeing on music, politics, personal likes and dislikes. She picked the red and green peppers out of the salad they had bought and he ate them while she decried his taste. They argued about who would have the last of the avocado, and in the end Reid cut it carefully in half.

He got her to talk about the new designs she was working on, and gave her the name of an Australian firm that might be interested in buying. He knew the manager, he said, writing it down for her. They fed the remains of the picnic to the gulls, pigeons and sparrows, and strolled through the park with his arm about her shoulders, and looked down at the harbour, watching the ferries and a few yachts on the Waitemata.

Then he had to fly to Wellington. Annys went to the airport with him and watched his flight leave, standing on the observation deck and waving long after the plane was aloft and he couldn't possibly have seen her any more.

From Wellington he phoned her every day, but when he came back ten days later he was on his way out of the country again. 'Europe,' he explained when she asked him where to this time. 'But it's only a short trip. Just the final check on a job I did last year. I've got one night in Auckland, so let's paint the damn town.'

He instructed her to put on something glamorous and took her to dinner in style. He looked very handsome in an evening jacket and black tie, and she told him so.

He grinned and thanked her, and said she was a stunner herself.

When he took her home the others had gone to bed or were still out, and for a while they sat on the sofa in the living-room, two cups of coffee forgotten as they went into each other's arms.

The coffee was cold when Reid finally tore himself away from her, running a hand over his hair. 'I haven't gone in for this sort of thing since I was a teenager,' he complained, picking up one of the cups and putting it down again with a grimace.

'I'm sorry.' Annys got up and walked away from him, going to fiddle with some photographs on the mantelpiece. She took a deep breath and turned to him, keeping a firm grip on her emotions. 'I'll make some more coffee,' she offered.

Reid erupted from the sofa. 'I don't want *coffee*!'

He came over to her, taking her hands in his, and in a softer tone said, 'You know what I want.'

Annys stiffened, looking away from him. 'Yes, I know.'

He waited, then sighed. 'I'm rushing you, and I promised I wouldn't. Sorry.' He bent and kissed her forehead. 'By the way, I have a clean bill of health,' he added. 'I'm well aware of all the dangers of foreign travel, and I don't take chances, ever.'

'It's not that,' Annys said. She looked into his eyes. 'I don't want to become involved with someone who... who might not stay around.'

Reid looked at her shrewdly, and nodded. 'I don't hold any records in that department,' he admitted. 'But there is something special between us, isn't there, Annys?'

'There is for me,' she said.

'For me too. Don't you believe that?'

'I think I do. I want to.'

He nodded again, looking down at their linked hands. 'Fair enough.' He looked up again. 'Annys, do you love me?'

She moistened her lips, part of her protesting, Unfair, he has no right to ask me that. Then she said, 'Yes.'

He put his hands on her shoulders and pulled her closer. 'I love you, too,' he told her, and kissed her almost reverently. Then he eased her away from him, and looked at her with a faintly brooding expression. 'We'll work it out,' he said. 'When I get back.'

CHAPTER SEVEN

ANNYS hadn't dared to think how he meant to work it out.

On his return, finding her alone in the flat, he took her in his arms and kissed her until she was dizzy with delight and mindless with need.

When he loosened his hold, he kissed her forehead and laid his cheek against her hair and said, 'I needed that, like a dying man in the desert.'

'Do you want a drink?' Annys asked, easing herself away from him. She could do with a little distance, some distraction, herself. She found it unsettling, this driving, inexorable emotion that was between them.

Reid laughed, holding her upper arms a moment before he let her go. 'What have you got?'

'Gin, whisky, beer. Some wine, I think.'

'Ice?' he queried. 'Whisky, then.'

When she'd got it he sat on the sofa beside her, toying with her hair as they sipped their drinks. 'Take me to see your parents,' he suggested. 'This weekend—I'll still be here.'

'It's a three-hour trip.'

'So?' He grinned. 'I've just come from a thirteen-hour plane ride. And before that I'd barely slept for sixteen hours.'

He was used to it, of course, but she could see now that he looked strained about the eyes, and under his tan there was a pallor.

She said, 'You must be *dead*!'

'Possibly,' he agreed. 'I did think, just now, maybe I'd died and gone to heaven.'

Annys laughed. 'Should you be drinking? Isn't it supposed to aggravate jet lag?'

'Haven't had jet lag in years,' he told her. But when he'd had two drinks, and pulled her close to him with her head on his shoulder, he sighed and murmured something into her ear, and fell instantly asleep.

When her flatmates arrived home he was lying on the sofa with a blanket over him, and Annys met them each at the door with instructions to keep quiet and not disturb him.

Four hours later he woke and found her curled up in an armchair with a book on her lap. But she wasn't reading, she was looking at him. The others had left the lounge to them, and she'd turned off the lights except for one table lamp at her side.

He stretched out a hand to her. 'Come here.'

She went immediately, knelt on the floor at his side and kissed him.

'Great way to wake up,' he told her, when she sank back on to her heels. 'Sorry I dozed off.'

'Maybe I should be insulted.' She smiled at him.

His eyes smiled back. One hand lifted a strand of her hair, watching it fall softly. 'Are you?'

Annys shook her head. 'You were very tired.'

'I'm not tired now,' he said, putting his hands on either side of her face to draw her down to him.

Several breathless minutes later she said, 'No, you're not!'

He laughed, sat up and swung her up on to his lap. 'Are you?'

Her eyelids flickered down. 'Not specially. But——'

'It's all right,' he said. 'I know.' He adjusted a cushion and eased her head down against it, then his hand began a slow, sweet exploration of her body from the rise of her breasts to the slimness of her waist, over hip and thigh and sweeping right down her bare calf to her ankle. On the return journey, he held her eyes with his as his hand slid under her skirt and along her thigh, then down again before she could protest.

'You have lovely legs,' he said. 'Gorgeous. Long and firm and strong. I can imagine them...'

As he stopped abruptly she knew what he'd been going to say, and colour flooded her face.

He saw it and grinned down at her. Annys made to struggle up, but he bent and put his lips to hers, coaxing hers open, and shifted his legs so that she lay by him, their legs entwined.

His kisses were languorous, almost lazy, as though he was content to have her close to him as long as she gave him her mouth. But after a time they changed, becoming insistent, passionate, probing. Annys wriggled away from him, slipped from his arms and stood up.

Immediately he was behind her, wrapping his arms about her, his breath in her hair. 'Where are you going?'

'Nowhere. I—just need a minute.'

'OK.' He nuzzled her ear, rocking her in his arms. 'Take it.'

Annys gave an unsteady little laugh. 'Let me go, Reid.'

Reluctantly he released her. When she turned, he was sitting on the sofa, one arm thrown across the back of it, his eyes regarding her with a thoughtful air.

She said, 'Why did you ask me to take you to see my parents?'

'I'd like to meet them.'

That didn't tell her anything. She looked away from him, and he laughed suddenly. 'Annys,' he said, and got up to catch her hands in his own. 'Annys, will you marry me?'

'Yes,' she said instantly.

She saw the surprise in his eyes, and laughed in her turn. 'You didn't expect me to accept?'

'I expected you to want time to think about it.'

She didn't need to think about it. The proposal of marriage answered all her doubts. He didn't want just a convenient mistress, or a temporary, part-time lover. She was important enough for him to commit his future happiness to her. He wanted her as a permanent part of his life.

And she wanted the same from him.

Her parents were impressed with Reid, but unhappy when he and Annys broke the news that they wanted to be married before he left on his next trip abroad.

'I'm going to one of the Hawaiian islands,' he'd told Annys, 'to advise on the building of a new wing at a resort hotel. I'll be living in one of their self-contained bungalows near the beach. It's a great place for a honeymoon, and we could hire the bungalow for a week of holiday before I have to begin work. And when I do, I hope you'll be waiting for me when I come home, just as you were when I flew back from Europe.'

As eager as he, Annys overrode her parents' objections. 'I'm twenty-four,' she told them, 'not a silly teenager being swept off my feet. I know I want to marry Reid; there's no reason to wait.'

So confident, she'd been. So sure that a man she barely knew was the one she wanted to live with and love for the rest of her life.

She had been remarkably naïve for her age, the older and wiser Annys decided. In spite of a couple of youthful episodes when she'd been sure her heart was broken, her various boyfriends had made no lasting impression. At university she had been dedicated to her study, and although she'd enjoyed herself in a closeknit group of friends of both sexes she hadn't wanted to be involved in any one-to-one relationship. She'd seen too many students lose their grip that way, coming to grief on the rocky shoals of starry-eyed romance.

And then her career plans had taken up most of her energy. Her father had spent all his life in a blue-collar job working for a large company, one of their longest-serving and most diligent staff. And when the company had got into financial straits, he had been made redundant ahead of several younger, newer men. Not ready to retire, he at first had declared his intention of getting another job. But he was already past middle age, and Annys and her mother had watched as discouragement and disillusion prematurely turned him into an old man.

It had made Annys determined that she would be independent, never working for anyone else if she could help it. Her teachers had consistently praised her ability, her mother and father were very proud of that, and early on they had started a special savings account for her education. Inflation had eroded its value, but when her father had got his redundancy payment he said, 'At least we can still afford to put Annys through university.'

She'd always come top of the class in school and done well in team sports and even better in athletics and tennis, and she'd continued her success at university. Her career choice had surprised her parents, who had vaguely pictured for her a future in academia or perhaps law or even medicine, but she had had other plans. After considering and discarding several options she had set her sights on running her own business, and her interest in both design and physical recreation led her to focus on a field that seemed made for her. There was, she thought, a need for clothing that was both attractive and comfortable for sportswomen and men, durable track and field wear that would allow them to participate in their sport with freedom of movement, comfort and safety, and know that they looked good at the same time.

Her designs were distinctive yet practical. Not only sports people but others who liked smart casual clothes were attracted to them. And she had just begun making a name for herself among those in the know when she had married Reid Bannerman.

At the end of their week-long official honeymoon Reid had to go and meet his clients. She kissed him goodbye lingeringly on the doorstep of their bungalow, and on his return she had a fresh salad and cold pork waiting for him. It waited a bit longer, because somehow the welcoming kiss she gave him led to their making love on the divan in the living-room. But for another two weeks Reid came home to Annys just as he'd wanted to, and she was always there to meet him, usually with a meal on the table.

Playing house, Annys reminded herself cynically, looking back. She'd known what it was, but perhaps Reid hadn't.

Annys moved to his flat in Wellington, and Reid said he could send other members of his team on some of the trips he used to undertake himself so he'd be home more.

She tried to keep herself free when he was home, because he still spent much of his time travelling. She would ignore the itch to get out her pad and pencils, tell herself she could do it when he was away, when she needed something to fill the hole left in her life by his temporary absence.

The first time he came in one day and found her busy drawing, pages of her sketching pad strewn all over the table and the divan, he'd just kissed the top of her head and looked interested in the designs she'd created, and suggested they go out to eat, it was time he bought her dinner.

As her designs became more popular, and her ambitions began to take shape, she wasn't able to compartmentalise her life in that way. Reid would cook or bring in take-aways when she had a deadline to meet, and then wait for her to come to bed and take her in his arms, and his lovemaking would ease away the tension that had kept her going until after midnight. When she had the chance at a cheap lease for her first boutique, he encouraged her to go ahead. The long hours she put in with her outworkers sewing up enough stock for opening day made her, for the first time, too tired to make love to him. And even then he just soothed her to sleep in his arms and said it didn't matter.

He had to go away the day after the opening, with an admonition to her not to work too hard. Irritably, she wondered how she was supposed to restock without working, because the opening had been a roaring success, and the stock heavily depleted. She had looked round afterwards with a small sense of panic, and known that she would have to find at least one more reliable machinist to keep up with demand if this was any indication.

She was conscious of a guilty sense of relief that Reid was going to be away for a couple of weeks. It would give her a chance to concentrate on the business at this vital time.

When he arrived back, she heard his key in the lock and as usual flew to meet him.

He whispered in her ear, 'Let's go to bed.'

But she hung back, saying regretfully, 'I have to finish this tonight, really. I'll make you a quick dinner and...see you later, OK?'

'I don't need dinner,' he said. 'I had a meal on the plane. I'll take a shower and go to bed.'

When she crept in beside him hours later he was fast asleep. She contemplated waking him, but she was exhausted, too. So exhausted that she forgot to set the alarm, and when she woke he was sitting on the bed holding a single red rose.

'You look beautiful, asleep,' he told her. He bent to kiss her, and she wound her arms about him, but in a few moments she moved her head and squinted at the clock. 'Why didn't you wake me?' she demanded, gaping at the time.

'I have now.' He bent to kiss her again, but she was struggling up.

'I have to see my pattern-cutter. I promised I'd have those drafts to her by nine.'

He looked momentarily impatient, but made her coffee and toast while she flung on some clothes, and she drank the coffee but left the toast. She went straight from the pattern-cutter to the shop and spent the rest of the day there, phoning home to tell Reid she wouldn't be back until after five.

'Shall I take you out to dinner?' he suggested. And, remembering his fleeting irritation that morning, she said yes, that would be lovely, thinking she was behind in her book-keeping, and she'd have to get up early in the morning to do it.

That was the morning he came up behind her chair a couple of hours after she'd crept quietly from their bed, put his arms about her and said, 'What ungodly hour did you get up?'

'Five. If I don't do this, I'll get so far behind I won't be able to sort it out when tax time comes around.'

'I could get my accountant to do it.' He massaged her shoulders absently.

'I can't afford an accountant, not yet.'

'You don't need to.' He kissed her neck. 'I'll pay him.'

'No. This is my business, and I'll run it on the money I make.'

'I love your independence, darling.' He bent and put his lips to her ear. 'But I love your body even more.'

Annys laughed. 'Reid, I've got to——'

'I'll help you with it,' he promised. 'Later.' His lips found hers, and he picked her up off the chair and bore her back to bed.

There was the time he phoned to say he was bringing some people home, and could she manage a meal for them? They were two Japanese men from a construction company that was planning to build a huge residential and commercial complex on Australia's Gold Coast. 'I want to clinch this contract,' Reid said. 'It'll be the biggest project I've ever had, and their preliminary designs are really interesting. I'll have to work closely with the architects. These people have been wined and dined at hotels and restaurants for weeks now—I think they'd appreciate a quiet evening and some home cooking.'

She'd cleared her work off the dining-room table and spread it out on the bed in the spare room, hastily used the vacuum cleaner and a duster, dashed out to buy ingredients for a dinner with a distinctively New Zealand character that she hoped was going to be appetising to Japanese palates, and spent the next two hours preparing it.

After the guests had departed, Reid returned from driving them to their hotel to find her immersed up to her elbows in dishwater.

'Why don't you leave that,' he said, slipping his arms about her waist to kiss her nape, 'and come to bed?'

And Annys snapped, 'Is that all you can think about?'

He stepped back. 'Is that a yes or a no?'

But she wasn't to be humoured. 'You go to bed if you like,' she said. 'I still have work to do.' She rattled another dish into the rack.

'Can't it wait?'

'It's already waited for——' she glanced at her watch '—seven hours. I should have done it tonight.'

'Look, I'll finish the dishes. Suppose you get some sleep and tackle the job in the morning?'

'Thanks a lot,' she muttered ungraciously, and stalked off to get her drawings.

When he came out of the kitchen she was frowning over them at the table.

'You should have said,' he told her, 'if you didn't have time to cook. I'd have taken them to a restaurant.'

'You told me you didn't want to do that.' She drew a line, muttered, 'Damn,' and screwed up the paper, throwing it on the floor.

Reid bent to pick it up and toss it into the waste-basket in the corner. 'We should fix up the spare room as a workroom for you,' he said.

'Sorry if I'm too messy for you.' She positioned another piece of paper and began sketching.

'Don't be silly,' he said shortly. 'Look, if you don't want to help entertain my business contacts, you can always say no.'

'Thank you,' Annys said with heavy irony. 'I don't want to entertain your business contacts, OK?'

There was a small silence. 'All right,' he said evenly. 'I won't ask you again.'

He turned and went off to bed without saying good-night, and Annys tried to blot out the guilty sickness in the pit of her stomach, and concentrate on what she was doing.

Maybe that was the first crack in their marriage. Reid was as good as his word, and never asked her to help entertain clients again. He would phone instead and tell her he wouldn't be in for dinner. Annys felt guilty but her work took so much of her time away from Reid that she resisted the impulse to retract her veto. She felt they needed every minute alone together that they could manage to squeeze into two busy schedules. And she could squeeze in more if she was able to work while he was with his business associates.

The Japanese-Australian project took a great deal of Reid's time, and he began spending days and weeks at a time on the Gold Coast. 'I can't leave this one to the others,' he told her, asking her to be patient. 'It's too important, and anyway our resources are going to be stretched to their limit. As it is I think I'm going to have to advertise for more staff.'

'It's all right,' Annys assured him, in the pleasant satiety they shared after making love. 'I'll miss you, but I know how you feel about being there.' Like her, he had to know what was happening in every aspect of the business. They were both take-charge people, reluctant to delegate unless they had absolute confidence in a person, impatient when they saw something done less effectively than they could do it themselves.

'Why don't you come with me?' He ran a finger down her arm, picked up her hand and nibbled gently on her fingers. 'Great surfing beaches on the Gold Coast. We could have fun.'

'I can't.' She shook her head regretfully, tamping down a faint resentment that he should imagine she could just drop everything for a spur-of-the-moment holiday. 'My boutique manager's leaving, remember? If I don't find someone for the job soon I'll have to take over myself until a suitable applicant appears.'

'Maybe you're too choosy.' He lay back and settled her against his chest. 'How many applicants have you turned down so far?'

'Half a dozen. I can't take just anyone, Reid. It's important to have the right person.'

'Yeah, I know.' He sighed. 'I'll get myself a Gold Coast beach bunny instead.'

'You will not!' Annys picked up a pillow and he fended her off, laughing, taking it from her to throw it on the floor. In the ensuing tussle they ended up on the floor too, wrestling, panting and laughing, until he had her pinned to the carpet with her head on the disputed pillow, and her hands held by his on either side of it.

'Give in?' he taunted her.

'Never!'

He settled his body closer, moving suggestively, his eyes teasing. 'Now?'

Annys shook her head.

His head lowered, his lips on her throat. 'Now?'

On a breath of laughter, Annys said, 'No!'

'Now?' he mumbled as his mouth descended lower.

Annys sighed and relaxed, her limbs going fluid. 'You don't play fair,' she complained.

'What's fair?' His hands moved, freeing hers, and she instantly grasped his hair with one hand and shoved hard with the other, reversing their positions as she straddled him with her long, strong legs.

'Now!' she said triumphantly. 'Do *you* give in?'

'Absolutely!' he assured her, holding up his hands in surrender. 'I have no defence against female muscle. Take me—I'm yours!'

Annys laughed and bent her head to his mouth.

She worked like a beaver when he was away on the Gold Coast project, making a special effort to clear the decks for his return. She hired Kate Driver as boutique manager, a little hesitantly because Kate admitted frankly she hadn't participated in sports since her teenage days, except for the odd game of social tennis. But she took a keen interest in her children's various sports clubs, and she had experience at selling and at keeping books.

It was a decision Annys had never regretted. Kate took so much of the workload off her shoulders that she began to think about expanding, opening another boutique in Auckland.

'Sure you can handle it?' Reid asked doubtfully when she mentioned the idea.

Annys immediately bristled. 'What makes you think I couldn't?'

'I didn't mean that. I just don't want you to get as exhausted as you were before the last opening.'

'I probably will,' she admitted frankly. 'But it's only temporary——'

'It went on quite a long time, as I recall. And you can't keep driving yourself like that.'

'Why not?' Annys demanded. 'You do.'

He paused for a moment, then said softly, 'We're not in competition, are we?'

She looked at him blankly. 'I don't know what you mean. Of course we're not. We work in totally different fields.'

'I'm not sure what I meant myself,' he admitted.

'You know what I think?'

'What?' he asked, smiling down at her as she approached him and wound her arms about his neck.

'I think,' she said, 'that, deep down, you want a traditional, submissive little wife, greeting you at the door every night with your pipe and slippers.'

Reid shouted with laughter. 'If I'd wanted that,' he said, 'I wouldn't have married a liberated, ambitious over-achiever like you.'

'Over-achiever?'

'It isn't a criticism,' he assured her. 'In my job, the last thing I need is a clinging vine sitting at home and fretting every time I'm out of her sight. I love your strength, your self-assurance. I know you're with me because you want to be, not because you need a meal ticket, or someone you can lean on.'

'So don't worry about me,' Annys suggested. 'I can look after myself.'

CHAPTER EIGHT

IN THE lonely night hours on anchor watch Annys found herself recalling the past. When had it all started to go wrong? When she had opened the second boutique and Reid had come home early from a trip to the Philippines, only to find an empty flat because she was in Auckland supervising the redecoration?

Or when she had arrived back a few days afterwards, tired and looking forward to falling into bed, and Reid had been entertaining a woman in their lounge? A woman whose blonde, blue-eyed prettiness was enhanced by clever make-up and an expensive silk suit that ought to have been businesslike but on her managed to look utterly feminine.

Reid had seemed to find his wife's jealousy rather amusing. 'Carla's an architect,' he told her. 'We've been working together, I had to come back here to fetch a blueprint, and I asked her in for a drink.' His eyes glinting, he added, 'And I don't expect to have to explain myself every time I invite a colleague into my home when you don't happen to be there.'

If she hadn't been so tired, and so disappointed, because she'd been looking forward to one of their passionate reunions, Annys might have reacted differently. But the hint of exasperated anger, the imagined accusation, fired her temper in return. She pointed out that to her knowledge he had never invited a male colleague home, and he rejoined that she'd made it plain she preferred not to meet them. He hadn't known she was coming tonight; he'd expected her the following day.

'I see,' Annys said, seething.

And Reid snapped, 'You damn well don't. This is stupid. I'm going to bed.'

'Don't turn your back on me!' Annys shouted.

He turned slowly and said, his face grim, his voice hard, 'And don't you yell at me!' His eyes ran over her, his expression softening fractionally. 'You look tired to death. Come to bed.'

She took that to mean she looked a fright. The flawless image of Carla the architect rose before her eyes. 'I'll go to bed when I'm ready,' she said. 'Don't wait.'

'Suit yourself,' Reid said, and left her wanting to throw something at his oblivious back, or burst into tears, or tear someone limb from limb, preferably Carla.

Annys gave a wry smile in the darkness, watching a silver ripple appear and disappear on the black midnight water. She folded her arms about herself, snuggled into a warm wool jersey, and pricked her ears at a small sound from somewhere along the deck.

Yes, she thought, maybe that was when the crack began to widen. For the first time when they were together they had slept apart on the big double bed. In the morning they had made love with a fierceness that yet held some hurt and anger. But it was after that night that she had unwillingly begun to wonder just what Reid did on those trips away, and who with? He was a very physical, very passionate man. Had he really been enduring long weeks of abstinence when he was away from her? Or had he found solace in other women's arms?

She'd tried to close her mind to those insidious thoughts, the tormenting questions. Surely she could trust him. He was her husband. She loved him. He'd never shown the slightest doubt of her integrity, despite the many times they'd been apart. How could she entertain such jealous suspicions about him?

Annys stood up, unable to bear her memories any longer, needing to move about. In any case, it was quite cold now in the dead of night, the sea cooling rapidly after the sun was gone.

For one thing, she answered herself as she stood at the rail, staring at the dark bulk of the land where they had anchored off the coast of the Coromandel Peninsula, he knew that he'd been the first for her. If she'd waited for him, she was unlikely to betray him with someone else. But one thing she did know about Reid was that he'd had other lovers. Perhaps had never stopped having them . . .

No use going over old ground—the gnawing jealousy that she had never again put into words, her determination to be a success, fuelled by an obscure need to show him what she could do, what she could be, and Reid's silent, tight-lipped cynicism as he watched her overworking until she became thin and hollow-eyed, her irritability when he suggested she slow down, and his increasing exasperation. The blazing row they'd had when he'd told her finally that she had to stop driving herself so hard, and she'd said he could tell her how to run her business when she took it on herself to manage his career.

After a while they had seemed to row more often than they made love. Until finally. . .

Annys called a halt to her thoughts. That door was firmly closed, something she didn't intend to think about, ever again.

Again she thought she heard a faint sound on the deck, in the shadow of the wheelhouse. She turned towards it, more for something to do than because she thought there was any cause for alarm. Something to keep the crowding, unwelcome tide of memory at bay.

A dark shape rose to confront her, and she gasped, startled.

'Annys!' Reid said, sounding almost as surprised as she.

She closed her eyes, giving her head a little shake to clear it. Her mind was so full of him that she almost wondered if she'd conjured him up. 'What are you doing here?' she asked him.

'Getting some air. Couldn't sleep. What about you?'

'I'm on anchor watch.'

'I see. I didn't recognise you when I came up.'

Wrapped in bulky clothes and absorbed by the past, she'd been looking out to sea with her back to the companionway. 'I didn't hear you,' she said. 'You must have moved very quietly.'

'I tried not to disturb anyone.'

'Considerate of you.'

'I'm a considerate guy,' he said, solemnly. 'Don't you remember that?'

'I wouldn't ask if I were you.'

He laughed. 'You have a different opinion?'

'Very.'

'Well,' he said, 'have you considered the possibility that I might have changed?'

Annys moved restlessly. 'This conversation is getting us nowhere.'

She was walking away when he caught up with her and took her arm. 'Where would you like it to get us?'

She turned to stare at him in the darkness, unable to see the expression on his face. 'If this is some kind of game——'

'No game, Annys. One thing about a sea voyage—even one as action-packed as the organisers have tried to make this one—it allows plenty of time to think.'

With her recent ruminations in mind, Annys felt herself stiffen, almost afraid that he'd been reading her thoughts.

Reid said, 'We never talked through our problems, did we, Annys? Every discussion somehow turned into a fight. And we only had one way of making up. A terrific way, but maybe we relied on it too much.'

That was true. In the end, it seemed they'd been totally unable to conduct a civilised conversation. Sometimes after they'd separated, she'd lain awake at night, feeling a piercing loneliness that he would never again lie beside her, and wondering what had happened to them, how they had managed to shatter the dream.

'Is there any point,' she said, 'in going over it at this stage?'

'Maybe. It's unfinished business, Annys. Don't you feel a need to understand what happened to us, to prevent the same thing happening again with a new partner?'

A new partner. The words brought an unexpected, piercing pain.

'Do you have a new partner in mind?' she asked him. She'd told him no one was waiting in the wings for her. She had as much right to ask as he did.

'No,' he said after a moment. 'No one specific.'

'Still playing the field, Reid?'

She had the impression he was frowning, but it was too dark to be sure. 'Something wrong with that?' he asked.

She moved away from him. 'Of course not. You're a free man now.'

'Irretrievable breakdown,' Reid said flatly. 'It sounds like a mechanical problem in a bit of machinery, rather than a marriage.'

Annys swallowed on a hard lump in her throat. She didn't feel like joking about it. 'I just want to be shot of the whole thing!' she said with repressed violence.

'I see.' His tone was clipped. 'No second thoughts, Annys?' he asked on a lighter note.

Her eyes lifted, trying to see him. 'Have you?' she asked incredulously.

There was a heartbeat's silence. Then he said, 'Some. I'm still powerfully attracted to you. And it isn't all one-sided, either.'

She made an impatient gesture of dismissal, and he said, 'Don't belittle it. Sex has made the world go round since the beginning of time. It's what marriage is based on, after all.'

'Maybe for you——'

His voice suddenly hard, he said, 'It wasn't any different for you. You hardly knew me when you agreed to marry me. You wanted me, and you didn't give a thought to the other things marriage involved——'

'That's not true!' Annys disputed hotly. 'You have no right to say it!'

'I'll say what I damn well please,' he said tensely. 'And you have no right to stop me!'

'I don't have to listen!' Annys swung on her heel, only to be brought up short by a hand on her arm.

She turned, blazing with temper, trying to prise it off, but his grip through the wool was implacable.

'You'll listen,' he said. 'For once, you will.'

She swung a fist, but he caught her wrist and wrested it behind her. He dodged her upraised knee and said sharply, 'Quit that, Annys. You won't get away with it.'

'You damn well let me go!' she said through her teeth, boiling with anger. 'Don't you *dare* hold me!' She made a furious effort to gain her freedom, but he wasn't letting go.

'I'll scream!' she warned him.

Reid gave a short laugh. 'No, you won't. You're too damned independent to yell for help.'

He would have been right, but just to prove him wrong she flung back her head and opened her mouth to do it.

Except that Reid didn't give her the chance. He didn't have a hand free but he stopped her with his mouth on hers, muffling the sound and sending a sudden white heat through her veins.

It was not so much a kiss as an assault, she thought, struggling to escape that merciless onslaught. Rage and desire created a potent mix, and she wasn't even sure when or how the battle became an embrace. She only knew that at some stage the turbulence of anger changed to equally turbulent passion, and the kiss grew in intensity until she could hardly bear the excitement building inside her.

She tore her mouth away, gulping in salty night air, hearing Reid breathing heavily in her ear. He still held her taut against him, and she bit her lip, to steady herself,

and turned slowly to look at him. He was staring back
at her, his jaw clenched.

Annys swallowed, and said, 'What the hell was that
all about?'

The fiercely controlled expression on his face cracked
only fractionally in a tight smile. His lips scarcely
moving, he said, 'Shutting you up.'

Annys said huskily, 'It seems to have worked. I'm
speechless.'

'That's a change.' Experimentally, he relaxed his hold
very slightly. 'I still want you, Annys. As I've never
wanted any other woman.'

'How many?'

He shook his head impatiently. 'Does it matter?'

She might have been top of the list—if she could believe that—but she hadn't been the only one he wanted.

'No, it doesn't matter now,' she said, suddenly weary
and depressed. 'It's all water under the bridge.'

He said, his hands loosening at last, 'You surely don't
think——'

He stopped there as they heard a footfall and Annys
wrenched herself out of his arms. Another figure appeared round the bulk of the deck housing.

'There you are!' the newcomer hailed them. 'I thought
for a minute the anchor watch had gone to sleep! I'm
relieving you, Annys.'

'Thanks, Wendy,' Annys said, keeping her voice
casual. 'Everything's been fine so far.'

As she turned to walk to the companionway, Reid
joined her. His voice low, he said, 'I want to talk to you
again.'

'It's no use,' Annys said. 'All we do is
fight and——'

'And kiss?'

Annys didn't reply, wishing she had been able to hide her instant, bewildering reaction when he'd kissed her.

Reid laughed a little. 'At least on that level we don't have a lot of trouble communicating.'

'At that level,' Annys said bitterly, 'animals don't have any trouble.'

'We're not animals.'

'Exactly. That's the point.'

They had reached the dimly lit doorway. As she made to enter, Reid shifted in front of her, blocking access. 'I resent what you're saying,' he told her. 'That's a cheap crack.'

'I happen to think it's true.'

'I don't believe you!'

'Believe what you like. And let me pass, please. I'm tired.'

Reid took a deep, exasperated breath. 'When can we talk?' he insisted stubbornly.

'Well, not here!' she hissed at him. Sounds carried at night, and she certainly didn't want Wendy to be a witness to whatever Reid wanted to say.

'Next time we go ashore,' Reid suggested. 'We ought to be able to find somewhere reasonably private.'

'We might miss out on some of the activities.'

'Damn the activities!'

'I paid for a holiday,' Annys told him. 'Including all those things. According to my doctor's orders——'

'What doctor?' Reid enquired sharply. 'You've been ill?'

'No, I'm not ill! I was advised to take a break from work. Prevention rather than cure. I'm supposed to be avoiding stress.'

'I see.' A moment later he said, 'I haven't been helping, have I?'

'Not much. It was certainly unexpected finding you on board. And all this—between us, it's hardly relaxing.'

'No,' he said slowly. 'I can see that.' He was silent for a moment. 'Annys, can I ask you to make a pact with me?'

Warily, Annys said, 'What kind of pact?'

'I'll back off, leave you alone for the rest of the voyage. No more confrontations. I won't insist that we talk. You finish your holiday in peace. And later—when we're back on dry land and you feel up to it, can we make a time to talk? Just once. We'll find some suitable place and sort ourselves out. Quietly, without recriminations.'

'Sort ourselves out? I'm not sure what you mean by that.'

He sighed. 'The truth is, I'm not sure either. I have the feeling that there's a lot between us that's never been said, that needs saying.'

'So that we can each start with a clean slate?'

He hesitated. Then, 'Something like that, I guess,' he agreed. 'Look, I promise I won't hassle you about it, if you'll just promise me in return that some time—within, say, two months of ending this voyage—you'll get in touch with me and let me arrange to meet you. Will you do that?'

It sounded totally reasonable, the way he put it. Why did she have this totally unreasonable sense of being backed into a corner?

'Are you sure,' she asked him, in a last-ditch effort to avoid the unavoidable, 'that this is a good idea?'

'Actually,' he said, 'I'm not sure of anything.'

Annys looked at him quickly. It was unusual for Reid, who'd always been so decisive, to admit to being unsure of himself in any way.

'I just have a strong feeling,' he said soberly, 'that I can't leave things as they are. We had so much, Annys.' And suddenly his voice was full of pain that found an aching echo in her heart. 'How did it all slip away from us?'

'I don't know,' she whispered. 'But we can't resurrect the past, Reid. We'd only hurt each other again.'

He made a movement towards her as though he would take her in his arms again. But Annys stiffened and shied away, unwilling to risk another earth-shattering physical encounter like the last.

Reid passed a hand over his hair and bowed his head. Then he stepped formally aside and said, 'I wasn't going to attack you.'

'I know.' His anger, and hers, had burnt itself out in that bewildering explosion of passion. She had nothing to fear from him. 'Goodnight, Reid,' she said quite gently.

She didn't hear his reply until she was halfway down the narrow stair. And then it sent a warm little shiver over her skin.

He said very quietly, 'Goodnight, my darling.'

CHAPTER NINE

ANNYS was glad that the next scheduled shore visit was one of the most demanding in terms of physical activity. She had tried river running once on a visit to the South Island and had thoroughly enjoyed it, but there were few interesting rivers in the north, and she'd not had time to pursue her interest in the sport.

Only some of the guest crew elected to join the rafting party, the others preferring a day on a beach with the opportunity of leisurely bush walks or fishing from the rocks.

The rafters were picked up by four-wheel-drive vehicles and taken along a rough private road for a distance of some twenty miles. Sitting beside Annys, Xianthe began to look pale after the first ten miles of snarling and bumping over pot-holes and ribbed slopes and around hairpin bends. Overhanging ponga fronds brushed the roof of the vehicle, and green and crimson ladder ferns toed the edges of the road.

'Are you all right?' Annys asked, watching Xianthe clutch her hard vinyl seat as they swayed around another bend.

Xianthe gave her a determined smile. 'I'll be fine.' But when they stopped outside an old wooden homestead she staggered thankfully into the fresh air, and Annys steadied her with an arm about her waist.

Reid came over from one of the other vehicles. 'Feeling seedy, Xianthe?' He took her arm. 'Here, let's find you somewhere comfortable to sit.'

They helped her to a reclining chair in the shade of the broad veranda, and Xianthe sank back into it gratefully, clinging to Reid's hand. He went down on his haunches and stroked a curl of dark hair back from her forehead. 'Can I get you something?'

Annys said crisply, 'I'll get it.'

When she came back with a dry bread roll and a glass of soda, Xianthe was already looking better, talking languidly with Reid. She sipped at the drink, ate some of the roll, and laughed ruefully. 'Sorry about that. Maybe I'm not cut out for a life of adventure.'

'You don't have to do this raft trip,' Reid said.

'Maybe you shouldn't attempt it,' Annys agreed.

'Oh, but I want to! I feel much better now, and I won't get sick on the river, I'm sure I won't. I'll be as right as rain when we've had lunch.'

They were served with lunch sitting at a long table set on a wide veranda, and then, carrying packs containing the inflatables and their gear, taken along a narrow bush track to the river where the rafts were inflated and put in the water, and everyone issued safety helmets and life-jackets to put on over the warm clothing or wetsuits they had been told to bring.

Tony gave them some brief basic instructions, including, 'If you go overboard, try to float on your back, feet first, so you can see where you're going. We'll throw you a rope. If you have to swim, use a backstroke to work across the current. Roll over only in clear water without obstacles. And don't go in after anyone who falls overboard. It's harder to pull out two people.'

There were three rafts, each carrying six people. Tony had Annys, Miko, Tancred and two other men, one a regular crew member, on his raft, and Reid and Xianthe climbed into another with two crew members and two other men. The third boat had only one of the Toroa's regular crew, but Annys saw that the paddlers included Jane and the other Japanese girl, who had proved herself capable of pretty much anything in spite of her size.

The first part was easy, the river flowing over shoals of smooth-worn shingle between banks lined with trees and ferns that dipped and dragged in the eddying water.

They had been given some practice at paddling in the sea, but manoeuvring around boulders and avoiding being grounded in the shallows gave them some moments of laughter and chagrin.

After a while the water was flowing faster, and the banks became steeper and closed in on them.

Tony, seated at the stern where he could keep an eye on all the paddlers and look out for trouble ahead, gave a list of clear instructions. Their boat was last in the line as they proceeded singly down the gorge.

Sitting behind the bow paddler, Annys could see Reid's dark head in the raft in front of them, and watch the powerful thrust of his arms as the current threatened to force them into a large rock in their path which the first raft had adroitly avoided.

She saw the other raft steer around it and then it was their turn, and she pushed with her own paddle according to Tony's terse orders, shooting through the gap and on into white water.

A little later they were resting their paddles and clutching at the side-ropes, leaving the two experts to steer while they enjoyed the sensation of riding the rapids, racing down the gorge and flying over a small waterfall to land safely at the bottom and go right on.

Fast-flowing water threw itself over rocks and bounced the rafts and their passengers as they wove about, slanting against the waves, curving round outcrops, jumping over a submerged tree-trunk. Whoops of excitement and squeals of mock-fear mingled with the rush and roar of the river.

Then Reid's raft went slewing aslant for some reason, and the water caught it and shoved it against a midstream rock. It tipped, and in that instant Xianthe lost her balance and flipped over the side. Annys saw Reid lunge to grab at her, but her weight combined with the angle of the raft was too much, and as the raft righted itself and careered on down the river they were both struggling in the water.

A rope in a bright plastic bag was thrown almost instantly from the raft ahead, the rope uncoiling as the red bag flew through the air, and the crewman in the bow of Annys's raft threw theirs, too. Reid had lost his grasp on Xianthe and was being swept along in the wake of their raft. He grabbed a rope but Xianthe had disappeared, and with her heart in her mouth Annys saw Reid look about, then deliberately let go the rope and, while the raft hurtled on, he dived under the water.

Immediately afterwards she glimpsed Xianthe's orange life-jacket in the swirling white turbulence. It wasn't moving, and Annys realised she must be trapped by some underwater snag. Reid wouldn't be able to fight the current to get to her.

Tony was swearing and trying to steer the raft closer. But they were going to go past before they could get near enough. Annys took a deep breath and, ignoring Tony's forbidding shout, slipped over the side.

Cold water buffeted her, hurling her against a submerged boulder. She didn't attempt to fight it, but breast-stroked diagonally with the current, heading for where she had seen the blur of orange. If she had gauged the direction right...

She saw a flailing arm and swam towards it. Xianthe clutched at her as the water foamed around them, sometimes right over Xianthe's head, the raft racing past in a blur of yellow, the paddlers unable to hold it against the force of the rapids. Gripping Xianthe's waistband, Annys tried to find the rope but that, too, was gone.

'Caught!' Xianthe gasped. 'My foot!'

Annys made a shallow exploration, fighting the determined pull of the water and hampered by her life-jacket and helmet, and could see the rocks that had trapped Xianthe's foot. She worked it free, and then surfaced, and with nothing to hold them now the water bore them along, not swimming but keeping their heads mostly above water.

'Try to stay with me!' Annys yelled against the roar of white foam splashing over rocks and hurtling between them. She still had a hold of Xianthe but was afraid that they could be wrenched apart at any moment. The power of the water was incredible—a lot of the time she couldn't see for the spray that kept hitting her face, and she had no hope of controlling their headlong progress along the river. She had never felt so helpless, so totally at the mercy of natural forces. What if there were more waterfalls? Even steeper ones? It was possible the water would push them under and they might never be able to surface.

Don't think about it, concentrate on avoiding the rocks, watching for calmer water, holding on to Xianthe.

She glimpsed Reid ahead of them, being swept along too but making a tremendous effort to reach them. Then he lunged across the current and was with them, shouting instructions that Xianthe gamely tried to follow.

It seemed an age before they hit a patch of slightly calmer water where the banks were rather less steep, and Reid and Annys backstroked across the current with Xianthe between them, to reach a group of relatively flat-topped boulders protruding into the river.

Xianthe yelped as they helped her out, and collapsed on to the rock, coughing up water.

'Thanks,' she gulped. 'I'd have drowned without you two. I don't know how to thank——' She coughed again, shivering, and then began to sob.

Reid said, breathing hard, 'It's all right, Xianthe,' and folded an arm about her shoulders. She put her head down and cried against him.

Half collapsed on the rock, Annys watched them, sawing in painful breaths of air herself. Over Xianthe's head, Reid said roughly, 'Are you all right?'

'Yes,' Annys gasped, not looking at him now. Further down the river the rafters had managed to stop their craft, and Tony and another crew member were cautiously making their way back along the rocky bank. Panting, she shakily stood up, waving to show that the stranded members of the party were safe.

Xianthe straightened up, still shivering. 'Sorry,' she gulped.

'It's OK,' Reid said.

'You're entitled,' Annys told her, 'after a fright like that.'

Xianthe looked up. 'You jumped in after me, didn't you?'

Reid shot Annys a glance that she found very strange in the circumstances. He looked blazingly angry. 'Yes,' he said, still looking at her. 'She did. Like a bloody idiot.'

'Reid!' Xianthe protested feebly, and started to cough again.

'You could have left it to me,' Reid was saying angrily.

Tony hailed them and landed lightly on the sun-warmed rock, closely followed by the other man.

A bandage for her ankle and a change of clothing was organised for Xianthe, and Annys and Reid too put on dry things. Xianthe declared she wanted to continue down the river, and once he was sure none of the three was suffering from hypothermia, Tony helped her back into the raft, to the accompaniment of cheers from the rest of the group.

Still standing on the bank as they waited for Xianthe to be comfortably settled, Annys glanced at Reid's set face. 'Are you OK?' she asked him quietly. He too had been swept into the water, they'd all been banged about a bit on the rocks, and he looked, she thought, a little pale as well as distinctly bad-tempered.

'Of course I am,' he said impatiently.

A fantastic thought crossed her mind. 'You're not mad at me because I rescued Xianthe before you did, are you? You couldn't have got to her, swimming upstream,' she pointed out. 'All the boats had already been swept past her.'

He gave her an incredulous glare. 'What on *earth* do you think I am? But since you brought it up, didn't you hear what Tony told you about rescuing people who went overboard?'

'*You* can't talk,' Annys retorted.

'I was already in the water.'

'You let go the rope.' He could have saved himself and left Xianthe to take her chances.

'It wasn't long enough for me to reach her, and they couldn't hold the boat.'

'So, what's different?'

'It was a stupid thing to do, Annys,' he said. 'Putting your own life at risk. When you'd been warned, too.'

'You'd never have reached her,' Annys insisted. 'What was I supposed to do? Leave her to drown?'

'It didn't have to be you. The crew is responsible——'

'They had their hands full. I'm a strong swimmer. I knew I could do it.'

He stopped, drawing in his breath. 'You think you can do anything, don't you?'

'Pretty well.' Her head went up. 'You told me once——'

'When I first met you. Yes, I remember.' He sounded thoroughly fed up, almost disgusted.

'OK,' Tony called. 'You two can get back on board now. We've managed the roughest bit,' he reassured them all. 'The rest of the way it gets easier.'

It did, the fast-running river eventually broadening into a slow, swamp-bordered sweep of water making its meandering way to the sea. The mishap had made them about an hour behind schedule, but by dusk they were back on the ship, and round a bonfire and barbecue on the beach later the rafters regaled the stay-at-homes with highly coloured accounts of their adventurous river trip.

Annys had put on a bikini and tied a flowered sarong about her waist. But although some of the party had swum before eating, she found she didn't fancy it, for once. Perhaps she'd had enough water for today. Xianthe evidently had no intention of swimming either. Wearing a sleeveless shirt, and jeans that hugged her slim, rounded figure, she was subdued, but told everyone that Reid and Annys had saved her life, bringing them a good deal of embarrassing attention before someone started to thrum on a guitar.

Across the firelight, Reid raised his brows at Annys, and made a small gesture with his head.

Annys gave an almost imperceptible nod, and quietly moved backwards, getting up to go to Reid's side as he walked outside the light and along the sand. He might be thinking better of his bad temper earlier, and she was willing to meet him halfway. He'd had a rough time himself, after all, and if he was getting fond of Xianthe her brush with death would have been a nasty scare for him.

She had to fight down a stab of jealousy at the thought. Xianthe was a nice young woman; she ought to be happy for them. Xianthe might be right for him, she decided, trying to be objective. She was very brave, and Reid admired courage. Although he admired competence, too, at least so he'd said. And Annys had tried to live up to that, had kept any doubts and fears to herself, mindful of Reid's stated aversion to clinging vines. She'd made her own way before and after marriage, never relying on him to help her out of trouble.

But he'd become irritated by it in the end, and when his ego had needed stroking, she reminded herself cynically, he'd turned to a different kind of woman.

Joining him, she said, 'What do you want?'

He hadn't stopped when she caught up, and they strolled along the sand, the sounds of laughter and talk fading behind them as they passed under the shadow of a tree growing on the bank above the sand. Somewhere in the distance Annys thought she heard the muted sound of a morepork's lonely two-note call.

'I figured you weren't enjoying the general admiration any more than I was.'

'True,' Annys admitted. 'So where are we going?'

'Just walking,' he suggested. 'We shared a fairly traumatic experience today. I felt like sharing something a bit more restful with you. Do you mind?'

Nonplussed, a bit wary, Annys said, 'No...I suppose not.'

Reid gave a quiet laugh. 'We could all have died, you know.'

'We didn't.'

'It gives one...a different perspective on things.'

'Does it?'

His laughter was fuller and louder this time. 'Always the pragmatist, aren't you?'

She felt a spurt of anger. Did he mean she was unimaginative, lacking some kind of mental spark? 'I don't see any sense in making a drama out of it,' she said.

'OK.' He shrugged. 'Subject closed.'

They walked on silently for a few minutes, towards a rocky outcrop looming blackly ahead of them, jutting into the water. When they reached it, Reid turned to her and said, 'Are you game?'

Scrambling over the rocks in the dark? It was probably crazy, but Annys shrugged and said, 'If you are.'

There was some moonlight, and the going wasn't as rough as might have been expected. On top the rocks had worn quite smooth but were dry and not slippery. Annys skirted a couple of black, shimmering pools and made her way carefully across to the other side of the outcrop. Reid didn't offer to help her, but she was conscious of him at her elbow.

Descending the other side, they found themselves in a tiny cove where the sand was soft and still warm from the day's sun. The tide was well down, and the water rippling over the sand left a gleaming patina on the deserted beach. A huge old pohutukawa growing at the base of a white cliff made a leafy cave.

Reid drew Annys into its shadow and said quietly, 'Let's sit.'

She sat with her knees drawn up, her toes digging into the sand. Reid spread his long legs out in front of him and leaned back on his elbows.

She hoped he didn't want to talk. It was very peaceful here, and she realised that this was what she needed, a quiet space for a while away from the ship where there was nowhere to be really private, and away from the strenuous activities for which she had previously been grateful. Grateful because they meant she didn't need to think too much, and they helped her to deal with Reid's constant presence in the background.

He was right about what had happened today. They could easily have died, and all day she had been pushing that thought and its implications away.

As always, she'd picked herself up and gone on with what she was doing, because that was the only way to survive.

She'd never been quite so close to death before. She had always enjoyed the adrenalin rush of dicing with danger—on the ski slopes, in the water, climbing—but had the sense to be careful and minimise the risks. She'd got a kick out of the experiences offered by this adventure cruise. And she knew that she'd been more reckless than usual because of some complicated, not quite rational desire to show Reid she was afraid of nothing.

She didn't know if that was part of what had made her dive in to go to Xianthe's aid today. She hoped not. It wasn't a very worthy reason. But there had been no time for thought. Split-second timing, which was what was needed before the boat went by and it was too late, didn't allow for soul-searching about reasons.

That came later. Like now. Remembering the cold shock of the water, Xianthe's frightened face, her own fear and helplessness later as the water had tossed them and hurtled towards an unknown fate, and then back to the sudden clutch of terror she had felt when she had first seen Reid fall from his raft and be swept under the white, roiling water, she shivered.

Reid said quietly, 'Are you cold?'

'No.' She wasn't really, but she found to her surprise and chagrin that she couldn't stop. She clenched her teeth, trying to control the increasing shudders that racked her.

Reid said, 'Annys! What's the matter?'

'Nothing! I...' She sucked in a breath. 'I don't know!'

His arms came around her, hauling her close to his warmth. 'Delayed shock,' he diagnosed. 'I got over mine with a stiff drink when we got back to the Toroa.'

Trying to stop her teeth chattering, she said, 'Maybe I should have done that.'

'Maybe.' He held her firmly, his arms wrapped about her, until the shivering eased and stopped. 'Better?'

'Yes,' she said, her voice muffled against his chest. 'Thank you.' He had put on a shirt over his shorts, but it wasn't buttoned up, and she realised her cheek was resting against his skin. She ought to move, but, breathing in the clean, once familiar scent of him, she felt a sweet lethargy, a desire to stay where they were, pretend for a while that the dreams they had once shared were still intact.

He moved, settling more comfortably but not letting her go, and one hand came up to stroke her hair. A tiny warning signal tried to make itself heard, but she was too tired, too lulled by the drowsy pleasure of his nearness, of the rare tranquillity between them, to heed it.

He brushed the hair away from her temple, his fingers feather-light, and touched his lips to the smooth skin, and she sighed against his chest but didn't move. When he shifted to lie on the sand, with her cheek still pressed against him, she didn't protest.

The hand on her hair slid to her shoulder and down her bare arm, and up again. His other hand stroked her back, bare but for the strap of the bikini top. It felt very good, very soothing. Little waves of pleasure began to follow the lines his fingers were drawing up and down her spine. Her eyes closed. She moved her hand, touching him in turn, her fingers brushing against a flat male nipple.

She felt the sudden rise of his chest under her hand and her cheek, and then, as she made to withdraw, his hand clamped hers against him. They lay there in silence for a few minutes, and she tried to tell herself this had to stop now. Only the last thing she wanted was to stop.

When he tugged gently at her hair to lift her face, she didn't resist, but as their eyes met she murmured, 'Reid, maybe we shouldn't——'

'Shh,' he whispered. 'Don't talk. Please.' And then he turned a little so that he could reach her mouth with his, and bore her backwards on the sand.

He was right, she thought, letting him open her lips to his. Talking led to arguments and anger, and this was what she wanted, needed, right now. The unique, unparalleled closeness and excitement, the affirmation of life that only making love could give.

She wound her arms about his neck and returned his kiss with a passion of her own, her open mouth an invitation, her body fitting itself to his in old, remembered ways. She let him unclip the bikini top and revelled in the touch of his fingers as they roved over her. She helped him untie the knot of the sarong at her waist and spread it on the sand so that they could lie on it. And she eased the shirt from his shoulders so that she could caress them and taste them and take gentle, nibbling bites at his salty skin.

When his hand stroked the inside of her thigh, she shuddered again, but with pleasure this time, and felt an answering tremor in him. She lifted her knee, and his lips replaced the stroking hand, and she murmured a sound of pleasure.

'You always liked that,' he whispered, coming back to her mouth, his leg sliding between hers.

'So did you,' she answered before her words were drowned in his kiss, while he pressed his thigh against her warmth, and closed his hands over her eager breasts.

She touched his hair, his shoulders, his arms, ran her hands down his back. She freed her mouth to gasp, 'I want you—now!' And parted her legs to accommodate him, then folded them about him, holding him tightly to her as he said fiercely,

'I want you too, Annys, darling! Like this, with your lovely legs around me, your arms holding me, your wonderful, strong body against mine, its firmness and its softness. I've wanted to be inside you again.'

'Oh, yes!' she whispered back. 'It feels so good. I missed you.'

He gave her a taut smile, holding back as she was, savouring the precarious, tingling plateau of pleasure. 'Missed being together like this? Lain awake at night thinking about it? How good it was?'

'Yes,' she confessed. 'Yes. So often.'

'Me too.' He kissed her mouth, and she strained towards him. He lifted his head to watch her as he moved slowly, deliciously, deeply. Her head went back, her lips still parted, and he dipped his head and put his lips to the curve of her throat.

For long moments they seemed suspended in time, and then she went rigid against him, and gave a small cry, and clutched his shoulders as wave after wave of ecstasy washed over her body, and she heard him mutter something incoherent against her throat, before she felt the quickened rhythm, the driving climax of his loving.

As it had always been with them, they were reluctant to relinquish each other, lying entwined and sleepy long after their need had been assuaged. When they separated, Reid touched her hair, kissed her lips with lingering tenderness and said, 'Want a dip in the sea?'

The tide had turned towards them while they were lost in each other's arms, creeping into the little cove, chortling around the rocks. They couldn't swim, it was too dangerous in the dark with so many rocks, but they walked hand in hand to the waves and helped wash each other, and then in silence returned to the beach and pulled their clothes on over their damp skin.

'Annys——'

She raised a hand and pressed her fingers against his mouth. 'Don't say anything now,' she begged. 'Don't spoil it.'

He took her hand and kissed the fingers, and pressed the palm against his cheek. 'All right,' he agreed. 'Not now.'

He held her hand while they negotiated the rocks, but as they drew near the glowing logs where a few die-hards still remained Annys loosened her fingers from his. Xianthe had gone, and although they attracted some covertly curious glances no one commented on the length of time they had been away.

CHAPTER TEN

IN THE morning Annys couldn't believe what she'd done. She'd slept deeply, dreamlessly, and had woken at first full of an inexplicable well-being. Then the night's events rushed in on her consciousness.

She stayed in her bunk instead of going on deck for her morning swim, not wanting to confront Reid again so soon, feeling she needed time to face him with a semblance of equilibrium.

A part of her was appalled that she could have been so weak, so willing to be drawn again into the golden net of desire; another part still tingled with pleasure whenever she recalled his touch on her skin, the feel of him under her hands, the sweet, drugging kisses they'd exchanged, and the ultimate closeness they'd experienced after so long an abstinence.

Abstinence for her, she reminded herself. She had no reason to believe that Reid had denied himself as she had. He'd had Carla to take her place. And who knew how many others?

He certainly hadn't lost any of his skill, judging by last night. Annys dragged herself out of a threatened slide back into dreamy reminiscence. Last night she'd been all kinds of a fool. Yesterday's adventure must have shaken her up more than she'd realised. And Reid had taken advantage.

Unfair, she admitted to herself. She'd put up only the feeblest objection. She couldn't blame Reid. What had happened had been wholly mutual, and she was as much a participant as he. She closed her eyes, willing the vivid, disturbing memories to go away.

'Are you all right, Annys?' Xianthe asked her.

'Yes.' Annys opened her eyes, saw that the other woman was dressed and daisy-fresh, apparently none the worse for her dunking yesterday. 'Just a bit lazy this morning,' she added, throwing back the covers.

'I'm not surprised,' Wendy commented, pulling on a pair of trousers. 'That was quite a rescue act yesterday. And you came in late last night.'

'Sorry if I disturbed you,' Annys said.

'Oh, no. I wasn't asleep. I only came in half an hour before you. I thought you'd already slipped off to bed before that, actually, like Xianthe.'

'I went for a walk,' Annys explained briefly.

'Bit risky on your own, in the dark, wasn't it?' Wendy asked.

'I wasn't on my own.'

'Oh.' The other woman gave a rueful smile. 'Sorry. I did notice Reid was gone, too. Only I thought you two weren't——' She stopped there. 'Me and my big mouth. It's none of my business.'

Annys looked at Xianthe, surprising a thoughtful look on her face. There wasn't a thing she could say without making the situation worse, she decided. She wasn't even sure what the situation was. Turning to pick up her towel and sponge-bag, she said, 'Looks like I'm late for breakfast. Don't wait for me.'

When she walked in she saw Reid look about for her, and gave him what she hoped was a casual smile before sitting down between Tancred and Miko. Afterwards they

both helped with clearing and washing the dishes, but
as there were three others on galley duty there was no
time for a private discussion.

The anchor was lifted after breakfast, and Annys kept
herself busy all day, surrounded by plenty of company.
By evening Reid had taken to watching her with a narrowed, somewhat intimidating stare. They made another
night sailing, but Annys went to bed early, pleading her
late night previously. By morning they were off
Whakaari, an active volcano set in the blue waters of
the Bay of Plenty. Lazy clouds of white smoke issued
from the crater, but the captain assured everyone that
major eruptions were not expected.

After he had checked that no significant weather
changes were likely to disrupt the balmy calm of the day,
parties were allowed to go in boats to the island, under
strict instructions to stay close to their guides and not
to disturb any birds or other wildlife, or the remains of
buildings they might find, left over from various commercial ventures when the collection of sulphur or fer-
tiliser had been undertaken from the island.

Avoiding a nasty-looking set of craggy stacks rising
from the sea, topped by colonies of seabirds, the flotilla
entered a small bay dominated by a high, sheer peak.
Where they landed, the meagre sand was littered with
boulders and driftwood, and the boats had to be pulled
from the water with great care. Ruins of buildings lay
about, and there were slopes covered in yellow sul-
phurous growths like flowers.

'You're standing on the lip of a volcano,' the voyagers
were told. It was very warm, and they could hear a rather
unnerving roar as steam from somewhere deep in the
earth's crust under the ocean burst from a fissure in the

rocks. Clouds of steam rose everywhere, and when it cleared they glimpsed thick, bubbling mud and gushing springs of boiling water.

Amazingly, there were wild birds and nesting sites on the island. Watching gannets meeting after one of the pair returned from the sea, stroking each other's bills and necks in a display of ecstatic affection, Annys looked up to find Reid standing a few yards off, regarding her with an ironic curve on his mouth.

Later they visited the other side of the mile-wide island and found young pohutukawa trees growing on the gentle slope. 'Nature will have its way,' Tony remarked amid the general exclamations of astonishment. 'Whakaari looks barren and dangerous, and you'd think nothing would live here, but it's not so.' He chuckled. 'The birds here have even learned that they can leave their eggs untended, and the earth will keep them warm.'

The visit to the volcano was their last adventure before the voyage back to the Bay of Islands. The ship headed northward under full sail, sometimes using the engine, and the return journey was made in less than half the time it had taken to sail south.

As most of the guest crew lined the rails to watch their entry back into the Bay of Islands, Annys felt a warm presence at her back, and then two hands descended on the wood in front and either side of her.

'At last,' Reid's voice said in her ear.

Annys stiffened.

'You didn't think you could avoid me forever, did you?' he asked her grimly. 'We have things to say to each other, Annys.'

'You promised,' she said, 'that you'd wait.'

'That was before,' he told her. 'Things have changed.'

Her voice deliberately cool, Annys said, 'Nothing's changed.'

She heard him draw in a breath through his teeth. He was silent for several long moments. Then, 'It has for me,' he told her flatly.

Stubbornly, Annys shook her head.

A hard hand turned her to face him, his other hand still on the rail imprisoning her. Seemingly oblivious of the other people near by, he was staring into her face.

Defiantly she met his angry dark eyes. 'You're making a scene, Reid. Leave me alone.'

'When you promise,' he said, 'to see me again.'

'What's the use——?'

'Annys!' he said with suppressed violence. 'You can't pretend that the other night never happened! It has to mean something!'

'It shouldn't have happened!'

'It did. And I won't let you ignore it.'

'I don't understand you,' she said. 'What do you *want* from me?'

'I told you,' he said. 'I want us to talk. What the hell do I have to do to get you to agree?'

'All right,' she said at last. 'I'll contact you.' Looking into his suspicious glare, she added hurriedly, 'I promise.'

'Fine.' He remained standing there and looked at her. Then slowly he let go and stepped back. 'Thank you,' he added formally, and turned away.

Xianthe was looking at them curiously. Annys gave her an absent, embarrassed smile and returned to her contemplation of the sea.

She didn't speak to Reid again, but when all hands were sent aloft to furl the sails she found herself next to him, efficiently rolling up the heavy canvas, the two of them working together in wordless accord. It gave her a peculiar kick of satisfaction, even though they didn't exchange a word or a glance.

On deck again he gave her a strange little smile and strolled off without a word. Xianthe came up to Annys and said, 'Are you and Reid getting together again?'

'No! Definitely not.'

Xianthe's look was disbelieving. 'You could have fooled me. And the rest of us.'

'I told you——'

'I know. And I still like Reid, I wouldn't have minded picking up the pieces, but not while he's still in love with you. That's a mug's game. Well, no hard feelings. After all,' she said, grinning, 'you found him first. Good luck, Annys.'

Annys was left gaping after her retreating back.

Not while he's still in love with you . . . he's still in love with you . . .

The words echoed in her head as she drove along the highway towards Whangarei.

It couldn't be true. She didn't believe it. But she was shaken by the intensity with which she wanted to believe it.

'Darling!' Her mother greeted her as though she had been away for years. She hadn't had time to call in on her way to the Bay, but was committed to staying overnight this time.

Her father ambled in from the garden that took most of his time these days, and kissed her cheek, patting her shoulder. She noticed how stooped he was getting, and made a resolution to visit more often.

She telephoned Kate first of all, who assured her that, 'Your empire has not gone into bankruptcy overnight. Everything's under control.'

Over roast chicken and her father's fresh vegetables, she gave her parents a brief run-down of the scenery she'd seen on her holiday, and of the less hair-raising activities. She'd learned early in life not to regale them with details of anything that might be considered risky. Throughout her childhood she had spent a good deal of time and ingenuity circumventing their over-protectiveness. She supposed it was natural in an older couple with an only child.

'Who else was there?' her mother enquired. 'Anyone you knew?'

Annys hesitated. She was never able to lie directly to her mother. 'Actually,' she said, trying to sound casual, 'Reid was.'

Her mother's enraptured face gave her a sinking feeling. 'Oh, darling! Why didn't you say? You've been holidaying *together*! Are things going to be all right now?'

'I didn't know,' Annys said. 'And we have not been holidaying together. It was a coincidence, that's all. Nothing's changed.'

She'd told Reid that, too. But deep down she knew it wasn't true.

Her father said, helping himself to more potato, 'Don't know why you two can't work it out. Your mother was looking forward to having grandchildren.'

Annys tightened her hold on the fork in her hand. 'I'm sorry,' she said. 'It wasn't possible.'

Her father looked at her sharply. 'Why? Do you have some kind of medical problem? You never told us.'

Inwardly wincing, Annys said evenly, 'I mean, it wasn't possible to work things out between us.'

Her father snorted. 'Seems a perfectly decent feller to me. In our day people didn't just divorce at the drop of a hat. You were mad keen to marry him. Told you to wait until you knew him a bit better, but you've never listened to us.'

Annys momentarily closed her eyes, remembering that this was one of the reasons she hadn't been here much in the past three years. Every time, they covered the same ground. 'I was wrong,' she said, trying to keep her temper. 'I should have heeded your advice. Now can we please change the subject?'

That night she dreamed about a baby, and woke with a familiar ache of grief in her throat. She could still feel the small, warm weight of the child in her arms, see the solemn dark stare it had directed at her. Had it been a girl or a boy? She would never know.

Impatiently she threw back the blankets and got out of bed, although it was only six o'clock. Her parents would be up at seven, as they were every day. She would disturb them if she went to have a shower now.

There was a mist rising from the smooth waters of the Hatea River, and beyond the town on the other side the bush-covered hills were a smudgy green. Whangarei had been built between the hills and the sea, and in summer that sometimes made for a sweltering humidity only intensified by occasional pelting Northland rain that flooded the gutters and left the pavements and roadways steaming. But mornings like this, cool and still with a promise of sunshine to come, were characteristic, too. For a minute or two she experienced a piercing nostalgia. It had been a good place to grow up, and once she'd had a fleeting thought that she'd like to bring up her own children here.

Mentally she shook herself. No use brooding on what might have been. There would never be children now.

Two months later she sat in a doctor's surgery, her mind in a turmoil of disbelief, shock and a slowly building elation.

Of course she'd begun to suspect, but had firmly forbidden herself to make any assumptions. Now it was confirmed, the test was positive. The doctor had just told her, 'You are definitely pregnant.'

She swallowed, feeling slightly dizzy. 'I can't believe it!'

The woman across the desk smiled at her a little quizzically. 'Believe it. Are you pleased, or is there a problem?'

'A bit of both,' Annys confessed. 'There'll be problems, but I'll cope.'

'Good. Your general health is good—I wish all my patients were as fit—but I'll want to see you regularly, just to keep an eye on things. You can make an appointment with my nurse in Reception.'

'Yes,' Annys said. 'Thank you.'

The first, most major problem was Reid. She hadn't seen or heard from him since leaving the Toroa. I'm not ready yet, she'd tell herself each time she thought about her promise to contact him. He said to wait until I'm ready.

When she got back to her office, the day's mail was waiting on her desk, including one envelope marked 'PERSONAL'.

She slit it open, and took out the card with a picture of Toroa in full sail. Turning it over, she read the terse message in bold black letters. 'Have you forgotten?' And underneath, two telephone numbers.

Forgotten? Not likely. She sat staring at the card for some time. Then, before she could lose her courage, she picked up the telephone on her desk.

When she finally got through to him, after waiting for his secretary to check if he could take her call, she said, 'I got your note. When will you be in Auckland next?'

He was so long in answering that she thought he had changed his mind. Just as she was about to suggest that they forget it, he said, 'I could fly up in the morning. Maybe we could have lunch, then go to your place.'

She didn't want him to come to her home, leave his presence stamped on it. 'Can't we go somewhere else?'

'I usually stay at a hotel when I'm in Auckland.' His voice took on a mocking note. 'You could come to my room there, if you like.'

'No, thanks.' It would have to be her home. And tomorrow was as good a time as any. She couldn't put it off much longer. Not now that she knew she was pregnant. That made it urgent.

She met his plane. She'd learned early in her business career that there was some advantage to be gained in a sticky situation by taking the initiative and meeting a possible threat early. When the opposition expected a retreat, meeting them head-on gave her the edge.

'This is a pleasant surprise,' Reid said, settling into the passenger seat of her car. It was one of the perks she allowed herself, a European car with a powerful engine and sleek lines. He didn't comment, but she'd seen the slightly surprised glance he had cast at it when she'd led him to it in the car park.

'Did you have somewhere in mind for lunch?' she asked him as she started the engine. 'I've booked a table at the Harbour View restaurant on Tamaki Drive, but I can cancel.'

He slanted her a glance, and she thought he knew very well what she was up to, but he only said equably, 'That's fine with me. Is it new?'

'Fairly. I've been there several times with business contacts. They give prompt service, the food is superb, and they have a very good wine list. Also a fair-sized parking area, which is a plus in Auckland.' She changed gear as the barrier at the entrance lifted to let them out on to the road.

'It sounds ideal,' Reid said. '*Is* there a harbour view?'

'Yes, from some tables. I asked for one outside on the terrace.'

'You've thought of everything,' he murmured. 'You're still terrifyingly efficient at everything, Annys.'

'I've never terrified you.'

'Not for want of trying, I sometimes think.'

Annys frowned. 'You're talking nonsense.'

He smiled, not answering, and Annys drove on in silence.

The meal was all she had promised him, and the view over the harbour was magnificent. Ferries drew white furrows back and forth across the blue water, and even though it was a weekday there were small launches zipping about under the Harbour Bridge and yachts with coloured sails flirting around a long container ship coming into port.

They talked little as they ate, beyond mutual enquiries as to how their business lives were progressing. 'I'm impressed,' Reid said, when she told him she was opening her fifth shop, this time in Sydney, across the Tasman Sea. 'Is this a good time to be expanding though? You're not afraid of overcommitting yourself?'

'My accountant is perfectly happy,' she said crisply. 'We've gone into all the possible pitfalls very thoroughly.'

Reid shrugged. 'Just a comment.'

She supposed she'd sounded defensive. 'I saw your Japanese-Australian project last time I was in Australia. It's quite a show-place. There was a shop vacant in the mall there that I looked at. It didn't suit me, I want to start off right in the city centre, but it's a fascinating concept, isn't it? Cradle-to-grave living, with everything laid on, no need to leave the complex for anything you need, except perhaps stimulation.'

'The theory is that all the stimulation residents need is right there.'

'I know. Libraries, sports venues, a theatre—but...'

'You'd want a change. Well, the residents aren't prisoners. They can go wherever they want, if having everything they need on tap palls.'

'Mmm.' Annys was looking down at her shrimp salad. 'I think it would.'

'For you. Some people need security more than they need stimulation.'

Annys thought of her parents, their shock and distress when the security of her father's job had suddenly been taken away. They had never got over that. They had not

been really happy about her being in business on her
own, but she'd pointed out that nothing was safe, and
they'd come to accept her choice.

She picked up a crisp pink shrimp on her fork, and
put it down again, swallowing on a sudden rise of nausea.
She took a gulp of her white wine, and then wished she
hadn't. It definitely hadn't helped.

Reid said, 'Have you seen your doctor lately?'

'What?' Her eyes flew to his face. Surely he couldn't
have guessed!

'You said your doctor sent you on that holiday. I must
say it doesn't seem to have done you a lot of good. You
look quite pale. I suppose you've been working yourself
half to death ever since you came back.'

'Actually,' Annys told him, 'she says I'm perfectly fit.'
Then she stood up rather suddenly. 'Excuse me a minute.'
Clutching her serving napkin in one hand, she walked
to the ladies' room, trying not to hurry.

Ten minutes later she rejoined him at the table, and es-
sayed a brittle smile. 'Sorry. What were you saying?'

'I was saying you don't look well,' Reid told her
bluntly. 'What's the matter, Annys?'

'Nothing, I'm perfectly all right.' She picked up her
fork again and toyed with the food on her plate. But
after a minute she had to put it down again. 'The shrimps
don't seem as good as usual,' she tried, shamelessly ma-
ligning the chef.

'You haven't actually eaten any,' Reid pointed out.
'In fact you've barely touched your meal at all. Want
to order something else?'

'No. No, thanks. I'm just not very hungry.'

She forced some salad and bread roll down, and made a pretence of sipping her wine. When the waiter took away her still almost full plate, she refused dessert, and Reid said, 'I don't need coffee if you don't. You'd rather go, wouldn't you?'

She nodded, unspeakably grateful, and he paid the bill without any demur from her.

He took her arm as they descended a flight of stairs to the street. 'What have you been doing to yourself?' he asked as she unlocked the car.

'There's nothing wrong with me.'

'Oh, yeah? Then tell me why you're as pale as death, and you couldn't bring yourself to eat a single shrimp— you always loved shrimps.'

'I still do.' Her stomach heaved. She never wanted to see a shrimp again.

'Shall I drive?' Reid asked.

That would only make it worse. 'Why? I just said, I'm all right.'

Reid gave her a look of extreme disbelief. 'Why don't you just admit you're feeling seedy, and be done with it?'

'All right,' Annys gave in. 'I feel a little off colour. Something I ate.'

'When?'

'I don't know!' she said. 'Breakfast.'

'You never eat breakfast.'

'My doctor said I should.' She'd been told to have something in the morning, for the baby's sake and to help prevent morning sickness. But this morning she'd been too tense to remember, thinking about what she was going to say to Reid. And this was the result, she reflected as she fought down another wave of nausea and started the engine.

'So what did you have?'

'Oh, for heaven's sake, Reid! What does it matter? It's none of your business, anyway.'

He lapsed into tight-lipped silence, and maintained it until they reached the white, Mediterranean-style house she had fallen in love with eighteen months ago. Purple bougainvillaea trailed across the archway between house and garage, and plantings of native shrubs softened the stark walls.

'Very nice,' he said, following her from the garage across the red-tiled patio.

She opened the door and ushered him into a cool-looking living-room with pale grey leather upholstery and smoked glass tables, warmed by the vibrant colours of an oriental rug on the floor.

'Sit down,' she said. 'I'll make you some coffee.'

In the kitchen she found some soda and downed a glass. The sickness was receding, and by the time she'd made two cups of coffee, one very weak for herself, and carried them through she felt almost normal.

Reid hadn't sat down. He was looking out of the big window at the roofs of the houses that ambled down the tree-dotted slope, and the view of more houses and trees with a distant glimpse of blue water.

When she put the coffee-cups on the table in front of the sofa, he came and took one and reluctantly sat down. She could have carried it across to give it to him, but she wasn't keen to have him standing over her while she sat.

He drank his coffee quickly, and for a minute she wondered if he was going to stand up again and start pacing, but instead he turned round, laid an arm along the back of the sofa and said, 'Why didn't you tell me you were pregnant?'

CHAPTER ELEVEN

ANNYS almost dropped her coffee-cup.

He couldn't possibly know, she thought wildly. She'd told absolutely no one. Not even Kate.

Her shocked eyes on his face, she said, 'What on earth are you talking about? If you're jumping to conclusions just because I've picked up some kind of bug——'

'It's no bug,' Reid said. 'You're pregnant. I'm assuming that I'm the father——'

'Well, maybe you shouldn't make assumptions!'

That brought him up short. His eyes were suddenly sharp, and angry. 'Don't play games with me, Annys. I know damn well you're pregnant, and I know it's my baby!'

Annys got up, backing away from him. 'You can't know either of those things!'

But Reid had followed her. He caught her arm and said, 'Look me in the eye and tell me I'm wrong, then.'

She looked at him and tried, but in the end she could only mutter, 'I don't have to tell you anything. And how the *hell* did you know?'

'I can see—I can't describe it, I guess it's hormonal or something. There's a look now and then, like a light going on somewhere inside you. Some women apparently have it when they're pregnant. It only lasts a second or two, but I've seen it before, and I never forgot it. You've always been beautiful, but it makes you breathtaking. It happened just now, when you came into the room.'

She was half inclined not to believe him. Yet how else could he have been so certain? 'Anyway, there's nothing to prove that it's yours.'

'You told me there was no one waiting. Are you telling me that you found someone in the last two months? Or that you got pregnant from some casual sexual encounter?'

'Yes,' she said. 'That's what it was.'

His face went pale and taut. Then he gave a short, harsh laugh. 'Is that how you think of it?'

'How else was I supposed to think of it?' she demanded.

'We were married at one time,' he reminded her.

It was Annys's turn to laugh. 'Legally we're un-married now.'

'Legally,' he agreed, dismissing the technical point with impatience.

Annys turned away from him. 'Anyway, it's not your problem,' she said dismissively. 'I'll handle it.'

Reid swore so loudly and explicitly that she swung about to face him, her eyes wide. When he reached for her, she flinched away from the rage in his eyes, but he had her shoulders in a hard grasp as though he would like to shake her. 'You bitch!' he said, his voice low and distinct. 'You weren't going to tell me, were you?'

She stared back at him, seeing an angry stranger, her silence confirming his accusation.

His grip fractionally loosened. 'How were you going to "handle" it, Annys? Did you hope you could quietly get rid of it without my ever knowing?'

'No!' That hadn't even crossed her mind. How could he have thought so?

'No?' His narrow stare was frankly sceptical. 'Why should I believe you?'

Annys blazed. 'Believe what you damn well like! I don't have to justify myself to you!'

'Who's asking?' he snapped. 'All I'm saying...' He stopped there, making an effort at controlling his temper. On a lower note, he went on, 'All I'm saying is that this concerns both of us, it's *our* child. And I resent not being given a chance to take my share of the responsibility.'

Annys mockingly opened her eyes wide. 'Responsibility? Now there's a new word for you! I don't need any money from you, Reid, if that's what you mean.'

'Let's cut the sarcasm,' he suggested. 'And I wasn't talking about money.'

'What *are* you talking about, then?' She moved experimentally, and his hands slid from her arms.

'I'm talking about giving this child a chance,' he said. 'Giving it a life. I know you're the one who's physically going to have to carry it, but I'll support you in any way that I can. And I know you have a business to run. Well, I can help there, too.'

'I don't need——'

'At least until the baby's born, Annys,' he urged her. 'Give me the right to look after you. Afterwards you can hand the child over to me. I'll take full responsibility from then on. You can walk away.'

Annys couldn't believe what she was hearing. Walk away from her own child? 'What on *earth* do you think I am?' she asked him. 'I'm not going to carry a child for nine months and give birth to it and then *leave* it! Not with you, not with anyone!'

'So what do you plan to do?' he asked tautly. 'You can at least tell me that!'

'I've hardly had time to make plans,' she said. 'I only found out yesterday. What I'm not planning to do is let anyone take this baby away from me, either before or after it's born!'

Reid's frown cleared, and he sat down. 'Well, that's a relief!' he said, pushing his fingers through his hair.

'I don't understand you,' Annys said, bewildered.

He glanced up. 'That's mutual. I find you totally baffling.'

Annys shook her head. Nothing made sense. 'You want this child. Why?'

About to say something, he suddenly looked away from her, his face closing. 'Let's say, I'm not getting any younger,' he hedged. 'And,' he added, apparently making up his mind, and casting her a challenging look, 'it isn't only the child I want.'

Me, Annys thought. He's saying he wants me. 'You just said I could walk away.'

His mouth was wry. 'I figured you'd find it hard to do that, once the baby was born.'

Impossible. It would be impossible, she knew. 'You play dirty,' she said.

He laughed. 'I meant what I said about looking after you—both of you. Think about it, will you, Annys?' He reached out and drew her down beside him, and sat looking at their linked hands.

Something very odd was happening. She felt a soft, treacherous warmth inside. She didn't need looking after, she reminded herself. But the offer nevertheless had a seductive attraction.

'Are you sure,' she said, 'that's what you want?' If so, he had certainly changed.

'Yes. Very sure.' Reid looked up at her. 'How are you feeling now?'

'Fine.' The sickness had quite disappeared. 'I hadn't been sick before, only I didn't eat anything this morning.'

He frowned. 'You do need someone to keep an eye on you.' He glanced about him. 'I could move in here,' he said abruptly, 'and be on hand to make sure you do eat something in the mornings, and don't overwork.'

Annys gaped at him. 'What?'

'Someone needs to,' he said.

'We're divorced!'

His eyes cooled, and he released her hand. 'I'm not suggesting we share a bed. I'll pay you board if you like.'

'Don't be ridiculous!'

'I'm assuming you wouldn't want to come to Wellington and live with me.'

'Neither of us needs to——'

'Well, if you won't move, I certainly will.'

'What about your consultancy?'

'Most of what I do can be done just as easily from here. I don't travel so much these days. We have some very experienced staff who can manage nearly all of that.'

He *had* changed, she thought. Reid had once been very hot on keeping all the reins in his own hands. 'Don't you have any—personal commitments in Wellington?'

He looked at her thoughtfully. 'If you mean a woman, no. I thought I'd told you, I'm not committed to anyone. If I had been, you wouldn't be in the—the state that you are now.'

'There's really no need for you to disrupt your life.'

'I'm not. I'm reorganising it slightly, that's all.'

'If you come here, people will think——'

'That we're back together. It's nobody's business but ours. Do you care?'

He knew she didn't give a toss what people might think. She could hardly plead a liking for conventionality. 'You know I don't,' she said. 'But has it occurred to you I might not want you monitoring my every move?'

'It occurs,' he said softly. 'I know how damned independent you are.'

Once he hadn't thought it was a flaw. 'I won't be bullied,' she warned him.

'I don't recall ever bullying you.' He smiled. 'In fact, I'd like to see anyone try.'

'You did,' she accused him. 'A couple of times on the Toroa, for instance.'

'Ah. You gave as good as you got. My definition of bullying is attacking someone too weak to fight back. And as I remember,' he continued, his eyes darkening in reminiscence, 'you didn't exactly want to——'

Annys looked away. 'That's not the point.'

'That's how we got to this,' he reminded her. 'It's never been all over between us, has it, Annys? Never will be.'

Not now, she supposed. Now they had created a new life between them, a link to the future, which bound them in some fashion forever. Part of her rejoiced in that. Another part was frightened by the thought of becoming involved again with Reid. There was too much pain and uncertainty in loving him.

Fatalistically, she accepted that she had never stopped loving him. That was why she was even entertaining the idea of letting him come to live with her, crazy though it seemed. It was why she had let him make love to her again, on the beach, without giving a thought to consequences, perhaps even welcoming the faint possibility of becoming pregnant. That fraught day when they had both been near to death; perhaps they had been driven partly by a need to reaffirm life. Perhaps the conception of this baby had not been as accidental as they liked to believe.

Reid said, 'What are you thinking?'

Annys shook her head. She couldn't tell him all that. 'I really don't need you——'

Reid stood up. 'No,' he said. 'You never have. I know that. But I'm going to be here for you, Annys, whether you want me or not. If not here, in this house, then as close as I can get. You're not going through this alone. I'll be in touch.'

She watched in stunned silence as he strode to the door and left, shutting it decisively behind him.

'Did you plan it?' Kate asked cautiously when Annys broke the news to her.

'No, it wasn't planned, but I'm going through with it and keeping the baby,' Annys told her.

'Good for you,' Kate said warmly. 'If I can help at all, don't hesitate, will you?'

Annys smiled gratefully. 'Thanks. Just knowing that you're in charge is a help. I'll be cutting down on my visits to the outlets, and putting a hold on developing new markets for a while. We're stretched as it is. What I'd like to do is hire an assistant for you, give you some of the work that I've been doing, and go back to concentrating on design myself. I don't want anything to go wrong with this pregnancy. Will you mind doing a bit of travelling?'

'Sounds fine to me,' Kate said cheerfully. 'The family's old enough now to cope without me for the odd few days. I've brought them up to be fairly self-sufficient.'

'I might need some advice on that, some time,' Annys told her. 'I don't have much experience with children.'

'Any time. Being a single mother won't be easy,' Kate said sympathetically, 'but I'm sure you'll handle it. Is the father... is he likely to be around much?'

Annys hesitated, then took the plunge. 'The father is my ex-husband,' she said. 'And he wants to move in with me. I'm not sure if it's a good idea.'

'Go with your instincts,' Kate advised her. 'You know, there are going to be times when you get the blues, wonder what you're doing carrying this great lump about for months on end. And you'll be tired. Before and afterwards. It's kind of nice to be able to unload on the father. No one else really wants to know, for one thing.'

Annys laughed. 'You're always so practical.'

'I'll tell you what,' Kate added. 'There's nothing like having the father there when it comes to actually producing the baby. Nurses, doctors, they're OK. A friend or relative, I'm sure that's nice. But the father—it's a part of him, just as it's a part of you. No one else has the same emotional investment. Gives you a great sense of partnership.' She smiled. 'Well, you'll see for yourself.'

A flood of emotion overwhelmed Annys at the thought of having Reid's baby with him by her side, both of them waiting to see what they had made together. Tears unexpectedly filled her eyes and spilled down her cheeks. Wiping them away, she said in a voice of muffled surprise, 'Sorry, I don't know what's the matter with me.'

Kate put an arm about her and gave her a quick hug. 'Pregnancy,' she said succinctly. 'It does tend to make us emotional.'

'Oh, yes.' Annys had forgotten that. She felt unnaturally fragile and vulnerable these days. She hoped the feeling wasn't going to last.

Maybe that was why, when two evenings later Reid turned up on her doorstep holding two suitcases and asked, 'Are you going to let me in?' she did so without a murmur of protest. It seemed too much trouble to argue, and if she was honest she really didn't want to.

'Where's your spare room?' he asked, and she silently directed him to it.

'The bed's not made up,' she said as he put down his cases on the floor and turned to her.

'I'll do it. Where are the sheets?'

She produced some from a cupboard in the hallway. When she bent to help him tuck them under the mattress, he said, 'I said I'll do it.'

'I'm not helpless.' She smoothed a corner and moved to the other one.

'I didn't say you were,' he told her, throwing a blanket over the sheet.

Annys pulled it straight.

'How have you been?' he asked when they'd finished. 'You look like a rose in bloom.'

'Thanks.' She glanced at him warily as they left the room. 'I'm very well most of the time. A little bit of nausea occasionally. I really don't need a nursemaid.'

He cast her an oblique glance. 'I promise not to fuss, if you're sensible.'

She might have taken offence at that. Instead she had that warm feeling of being cared for. She said, 'Do you want a drink or something?'

'Coffee,' he said. 'I'll get it.'

Annys waited for him in one of the deep chairs. He handed her a cup, coffee made the way she usually liked it. She sat with her legs curled under her, sipping it. Outside darkness was falling, and lights came on in the houses. She ought to draw the curtains, but she felt too lazy.

'Do you mind if I give your phone number to some people who may need to contact me?' he asked her.

'Feel free.' She sipped at the drink. She wondered if she ought to cut down for the baby's sake. 'I often work with the answering machine switched on,' she warned him. 'They may have to leave a message.'

'I'll be in our Auckland office most of the day. I'll answer all calls in the evenings, if you like.'

She thought about that. 'I haven't told my parents yet,' she said.

'About me being here? Or about the baby?'

'Both. Neither. My mother will be pleased. She wants a grandchild.'

'You didn't think of that before?'

Annys flicked a glance at him. 'What was I supposed to do?'

He looked grim. Then he shrugged. 'OK, let's not open old wounds.'

She wasn't sure what he meant by that, but it seemed a good principle to abide by. He'd hardly walked in the door, and she was taking an extraordinary and rather shameful pleasure in having him here, sitting opposite her with his jacket and tie off, appearing relaxed and at home. She certainly didn't want to start any rows.

'We could drive up at the weekend and visit them, if you like,' Reid suggested.

'I'll think about it.' She wasn't sure if she was ready for that. Her parents would assume this meant that her marriage to Reid was all on again. Annys was still feeling her way.

She ran a finger round the rim of her cup, thinking.

'Finished?' Reid asked, standing up.

'No.' She drank the rest and made to get up, but he held out his hand for it. 'Don't move.'

Bemused, she watched him go to the kitchen. When he came back she said, 'Maybe I could get used to this treatment. Is it your intention to spoil me rotten?'

Still on his feet, he smiled down at her. 'Isn't that the accepted treatment for expectant mothers? Outlandish snacks in the middle of night, their every whim indulged?'

'Sounds good to me.' Annys uncurled her legs and stretched, a hand lifting her hair from her neck. 'How come I never got this treatment before?'

Reid's smile died. A brief flash of awareness lit his eyes as he watched her. 'I don't think you wanted it before,' he said. 'Did you?'

Not that she'd ever admitted, Annys acknowledged silently. Aloud she said, 'You never asked, did you?' She stood up, facing him.

'My mistake?' he said on a soft, querying note.

'Maybe.'

She had a strange impression that he was almost holding his breath. 'Tell me more,' he said.

But she was afraid now. Afraid of breaking the precarious peace between them. Anything, she thought, could tip that delicate balance. 'I'm tired,' she said. 'I know it's early, but I've been going to bed early a lot lately.'

'We never had that talk.'

'You want to talk now?'

'Not if you're tired,' he said very evenly. 'There's plenty of time. I'm going to be here for a while.'

How long was a while? she wondered. Until the baby was born, he had implied. And afterwards, did he plan on sticking around? Maybe he was leaving that decision until later. He had said he wanted to give the child a father, but that didn't necessarily mean they must be living in the same house.

So many unanswered questions. Questions on the future. Questions from the past.

In the middle of the night she had to get up. That was another symptom she had forgotten about. There was a light under the spare-room door. On her way back to her bedroom she heard a sudden thump, and a grunt.

She hesitated. It was one o'clock in the morning. She tapped on the door, then opened it.

Reid lay on the bed, still dressed in trousers and shirt, although he had undone most of the buttons on the shirt. He was surrounded by files and papers, and held a hefty folder in his hand.

He looked at her, dressed in a thin silk wrap over her nightgown, and a faint smile hovered on his mouth. 'Dare I hope this is an invitation?'

'I heard something . . . but you're obviously all right.'

'I dropped this.' He lifted the folder in his hand. 'Sorry, did I wake you?'

'I needed the bathroom. Are you working?'

'Good guess.' He looked around at the cluttered bed. 'If you *were* issuing invitations,' he said hopefully, 'I could move it.'

Annys shook her head. 'You could use my workroom in future,' she said. 'There's a desk in there.'

'Thank you. Sure I won't be in your way?'

'Not at this time of the night. I've given up burning midnight oil.'

'Have you? Pity you didn't do so a bit earlier. When we were still married.'

'All the time we were married I had to juggle my time to fit in with you.'

Reid put down the folder, shoved aside some papers and stood up, coming towards her.

'How's that again?'

'Never mind. I didn't mean to dredge it up now.'

'You're saying that it was my fault you worked impossible hours?'

'I'm not saying it was anyone's fault,' Annys protested. 'I just said that it needed to be done.'

'And fitted around my supposed needs? Is that really what you were doing?'

'Often, yes.' She faced him stubbornly. 'I tried to allow time for us to be together.'

'I was trying, too, Annys. So how did we lose the lines of communication after all?'

'I... don't know,' she said. 'But at the end they just weren't there, were they?'

She looked at him sadly, and saw an answering sadness in his eyes. Surprised, she said, 'Did you really care?'

His reply came slowly. 'If you don't know that, then we had really lost each other. What on earth could make you think for a minute that I didn't care?'

'Well, if you did,' she cried, all the remembered pain and anger suddenly surging together and spilling out, 'why were you making love to Carla?'

CHAPTER TWELVE

REID looked absolutely astounded. 'Why was I *what*?'

'You thought I didn't know,' Annys said, 'but I saw
you with her. If you're looking for reasons, Reid, try
that. I'm not such a fool as you thought.'

'I never thought you were, until this moment,' Reid
said, his voice harsh. 'What exactly are you accusing me
of?'

'I just told you! I saw you together.'

'We were together quite often,' Reid said. 'You know
we worked together on several projects. That doesn't
make me an adulterer!'

'You weren't working when I saw you——'

'Wait a minute,' Reid said slowly. 'Tell me what you
saw. When—and where. You do remember?' he added
sarcastically, as she hesitated.

'Vividly,' Annys snapped. The scene was painfully
etched on her memory. She would never be able to forget
it.

They'd had a row the night before. She'd woken late,
feeling muzzy and sick. For the first time ever Reid had
left their bed, and the house, without saying goodbye
to her.

She had looked for a note, or some sign from him.
There had been nothing. She'd made herself breakfast,
listlessly, and tried to interest herself in some work in
the room they had converted from a spare bedroom. And
found herself sitting with a pencil in her hand, staring

into space and wondering what it was that had gone so wrong with their marriage.

The sickness that usually faded after breakfast had persisted that morning, and she'd had to leave her drawing table and hurry to the bathroom. Afterwards she hadn't gone back to work, but had lain on the bed for a while. She had been eight weeks pregnant, and with her hand on her stomach she could feel the slight roundness that as yet hardly showed, although the test kit she had bought from a chemist had definitely shown positive.

Her mind had gone back to the night before, when she had told Reid about the baby. She had closed her eyes, holding back tears.

Nothing had gone quite as she'd planned it. She'd cooked a special meal, but he'd phoned to say he was held up and not to wait for him. In the end she'd emptied the meal down the waste disposal. It wasn't the kind of thing that kept well, and she'd only eaten a little herself before nausea had risen in the throat and she couldn't swallow any more.

When he finally came in she was in bed with the light out, but she turned as he entered the bedroom, ready with a smile for him.

He didn't see it, because he didn't switch on the light. 'Sorry,' he said. 'Did I wake you?'

'I wasn't asleep.'

She waited for him as he undressed in the dark and slipped in beside her. He lay on his back, a foot away from her, and propped an arm behind his head, letting out a long sigh.

'Heavy day?' Annys asked.

'You could say that. How was yours?'

'All right. I didn't get much work done. I ... went to the doctor.'

'What's the matter?' he asked, quickly swivelling his head to look at her.

'Well,' Annys said, trying to sound casual, 'nothing, really. I'm pregnant.'

Reid was silent and still for a long time. So long that her heart began to die inside her. Obviously the news didn't bring him any pleasure. Then he said, his voice flat and expressionless, 'You're what?'

'Pregnant,' she said, her own voice rising with tension, because the news that had filled her with joyful trepidation was being greeted so curtly. 'As in with child. Going to have a baby!'

Again he seemed to hesitate. 'Did you ... plan it?'

'No, of course I didn't plan it!' Did he think she'd have done that without consulting him?

'I see,' Reid said. 'So it's not something you meant to happen.'

'I didn't do it on my own,' she said. 'You're partly responsible too, you know!'

'I'm not denying responsibility,' he said. 'So. It isn't the end of world. Inconvenient, maybe——'

'Inconvenient!' Annys wanted to howl, or hit him. Was that all it meant to him? An inconvenience?

They had only once discussed the possibility of having children, in some vaguely foreseen future. There was no hurry, they'd agreed. Annys was at the start of a promising career, Reid was heavily involved with his which often took him away on business, and they wanted time with each other first.

'We'll get round it,' Reid assured her. 'We can afford to pay for good childcare. Maybe even a nanny. You won't have to give up your work, though it'll take a bit of adjusting.'

Driven by an obscure sense of outrage that he was already consigning their unborn child to the care of strangers, trying to minimise the *inconvenience*, Annys said, seething, 'And what adjustments will *you* be making? Or am I supposed to make them all?'

'Not at all.' His voice was cool and even. 'I was planning anyway to cut down on my overseas trips,' he said. 'We've just headhunted a very promising young engineer. He's single, with no family commitments. I'm hoping to groom him to take my place on some projects. I thought that you and I could have more time together, just the two of us.'

'It won't be just the two of us,' she reminded him. 'And baby makes three, remember?'

'I haven't forgotten. All the more reason for me to be around. If our family is going to arrive sooner rather than later, well ... it's not a tragedy.'

'Just a disaster?' Annys said sarcastically. Obviously that was how he thought of it, something that had to be 'got round'.

'It doesn't need to be. How are you feeling?'

'I *was* feeling fine,' Annys said bitterly. 'Considering I've still got seven months to go. You're not helping much.' She was feeling sick now, with disappointment at his grudging acceptance.

Reid said, 'Look, we're heading for another row, and that won't help much, either. I know you're fed up with me at the moment. And frankly, I'm dead tired. It *has* been a long and difficult day.'

'Sorry if I added to it,' Annys said stiffly. 'I suppose this has been the last straw.'

'Don't be silly,' Reid said wearily. 'I'm glad you told me.' He reached out and found her hand, holding it tightly for a moment. 'And I'm sorry I can't entirely share your feelings. Let's sleep on it, shall we?'

'It won't go away by morning,' Annys said resentfully.

She wished passionately that he would take her in his arms and assure her that really he was delighted. Instead, he leaned over and gave her a light kiss on the forehead and said, 'Go to sleep.'

She wanted to, but she lay awake for hours instead, going over the conversation, listening to Reid's steady breathing, and getting more and more depressed.

And in the morning she could scarcely believe that he'd left without a word. Lying on the bed while the sickness receded, wondering if the faint fluttering she felt in her stomach could possibly be her baby's movements, although she believed it was far too soon, she came to a decision. They had to make time for each other, she and Reid. And they'd have to do it before the baby was born. Because if they hadn't sorted out their problems by then, things would only get worse. Always their times together were snatched from their commitment to their jobs. A baby would take more time, leaving them even less for each other.

Last night Reid had said he was already making some move towards resolving that. He'd been expressing a willingness to alter his life for her, and he was willing, if not eager, to include the baby. In her disappointment over his reaction to her momentous news, she'd brushed that aside. And that wasn't fair. She owed it to him and to their marriage to make up for it and meet him halfway.

And maybe he'd have had time by now to come to terms with his impending fatherhood and begin to look forward to it, rather than accept it as something that must be dealt with in the best way possible.

She was feeling better by the minute, and as she dressed carefully in one of her most flattering dresses, smoothing it anxiously over her stomach, slipping her feet into high-heeled sandals that she seldom wore, she planned how she would kidnap him from his office and take him out to lunch. It was a long time since they'd done that, and usually it had been Reid who'd called in on her and persuaded her to abandon work for a proper, leisurely meal.

Maybe they'd take a stroll afterwards along the waterfront, maybe they'd even go back to the apartment and spend an hour or so in bed, as they used to sometimes, scrambling into their clothes afterwards to return late to their respective desks, and working overtime in the evening to make up for their truancy.

Her step quickened as she entered the lobby of his office building, and instead of taking the lift she ran lightly up two flights of stairs, arriving at his floor pink-cheeked and breathing a little quickly.

She stopped to regain her poise, and a woman hurrying past to the lift gave her the faint, puzzled smile of someone who'd seen her before but didn't recall her name. Annys had reached the outer office of Bannerman International before the penny dropped and she remembered who the woman was. The receptionist, of course. They'd met only once—Annys didn't often drop into Reid's office.

Guiltily she began planning to take more interest in Reid's business. She'd suggest that if he gave her warning she'd be pleased to entertain clients or associates with him. Giving up an occasional evening for that wouldn't hurt her.

She walked down the wide carpeted corridor to the glass door that stood open. The receptionist's desk was empty. Three doors opened off the reception area. The one with Reid's name printed on it in black lettering was not quite closed. She pushed it wider and stopped in the doorway, transfixed with shock.

Behind the desk, Reid was seated in his large swivel chair, turned slightly to one side. He had his arms clasped tightly about a slim blonde woman who stood in front of him with her back almost to the door. Carla. Her head was bent, one hand stroking Reid's hair, the other on his shoulder, and his face was buried in the front of her blouse, half hidden by her lilac linen jacket.

Neither of them looked up. They hadn't heard her. Then Reid murmured something incoherent, and Carla whispered, 'Oh, Reid! My dear!'

Annys backed away, her mind reeling. She almost ran from the office, and along the corridor. The lift, she saw, glancing at the red light on the wall, was up on the sixth floor. Anyway, she didn't want to be locked in a small box with other people.

She fled down the stairs, running faster and faster, thinking of nothing but getting away as quickly as possible.

She was approaching the last landing when one of her high heels slipped on the marble surface, and she turned her foot and fell down the final half-dozen stairs, landing heavily with a sickening jolt.

Shakily she picked herself up, and limped down the rest of the flight holding on to the railing, trying to steady her breathing.

Carla. 'We work together a lot,' Reid had told her. Was she the real reason he wanted to spend more time in New Zealand rather than abroad? Not Annys, certainly not the baby, which he'd only found out about last night.

No wonder he'd been less than overjoyed. Perhaps, she thought in sudden panic, he had been planning to divorce Annys and marry Carla? Or did he want to have his cake and eat it? Annys *and* Carla. And how many others?

She walked all the way home, sometimes in a blank daze, sometimes with her thoughts in such chaos that she nearly stepped on to the road in front of a bus and, terrified, pulled herself together. The baby, she'd thought in that instant of danger. Never mind her life; there was another life to consider now.

When she got home and unlocked the front door she found she was very tired. And something else impinged on her consciousness. Her emotional confusion and anguish had been such that the physical symptoms had seemed just a part of it. But now it dawned on her that for some time there had been a dragging pain in her groin. She lay on the sofa and closed her eyes and willed the pain to go away, but it got worse, and at last she couldn't ignore it.

She didn't have a regular doctor, had never needed one. She looked in the Yellow Pages with fumbling fingers and found the number of a private twenty-four-hour outpatients' clinic. The nurse said, 'Can you get a taxi and come in?'

When she came home hours later, Reid was there. He got up from the sofa where he'd been sitting and said, 'Where have you been? I called the shop—you look terrible!'

They had wanted to book her into hospital overnight, but it was all over now, and she'd insisted on coming home. They'd given her pain-killers and other pills and told her to phone if she was worried. She'd already had some pills at the clinic, and they'd left her a bit light-headed. The staff had made her assure them that she wouldn't try to drive. They'd been a bit happier when she'd asked them to call her a taxi, and told them her husband would be at home.

'I'll be OK,' she told Reid. She was confused, fool-ishly surprised to find he looked just the same. She had been inspecting his face for signs of his betrayal.

'Where have you been?' he asked her again.

'At a clinic,' she said, the words sounding disem-bodied, unreal. She felt ready to drop at his feet with sheer weariness.

'The baby?' he queried sharply, taking a quick step towards her. 'Is everything all right?'

'There isn't going to be any baby,' Annys said starkly. 'Not any more.' Then, as the room swayed gently around her, she added, 'I really have to go to bed.' She ignored the hand he had been extending to her and walked out of the room.

She heard him say, '*What*?' But she was already grimly making her way down the passageway to the bedroom.

He had followed her. 'What are you talking about, Annys? What have you *done*?' But the questions seemed very distant, and struggling out of her dress and shoes took all her energy. She had none left to answer him.

After she'd crawled between the sheets in her underwear, she was dimly aware of him shaking her, of his voice somewhere far away. 'Sorry,' she muttered. 'They gave me some pills...' And then she slid into blessed sleep.

When she woke there was light shining on her closed eyelids, and a waiting silence, and she felt like nothing. A curiously empty, weightless sensation assailed her, followed by a piercing dread and then a gut-wrenching, thundering depression.

She knew that Reid was in the room before she opened her eyes, in spite of his stillness. Her lids lifted slowly, and she saw him standing by the window. He looked as though he hadn't been to bed. His hair was untidy and his cheeks shadowed, his shirt rumpled.

He turned his head and came over to the bed. 'How do you feel?' he asked her. His face was austere, as though he was holding himself in.

'All right.' It wasn't true, but the last thing she wanted was Reid's pity. 'Shouldn't you be at the office?'

'Later. Want to talk about it?'

Annys shook her head, looking away from him. She didn't want to talk about anything to him. He hadn't wanted the baby, anyway. Was probably relieved.

'You still look terrible,' he said. 'Can I get you anything?'

'No.' She wouldn't look at him. 'Please go away, Reid. I'd rather be alone.'

'If that's what you want.' He paused. 'I'll make you a cup of tea. You don't have to drink it.'

He left it on the bedside table minutes later. 'Call me at the office if you need anything,' he told her. 'You look as though you'd better stay in bed.'

She managed to say, 'Thank you,' and then he was gone. He hadn't kissed her goodbye, she thought, and foolishly, weakly, she began to cry.

Later she'd dragged herself from the bed and packed a couple of suitcases, written Reid a brief note and left.

CHAPTER THIRTEEN

'I REMEMBER it vividly,' Annys had just told Reid, three years later. She drew her wrap tighter about her body, standing very straight. The reading lamp he had been using cast a glow over her spare-room bed behind him, leaving his face in shadow. 'It was the day before I...left you. I went to see you at your office, and your receptionist had just gone out—for lunch, I suppose. You and Carla were there, sharing what I can only describe as an intimate embrace.'

Reid said, 'We didn't see you.' She saw that he remembered. There was a flicker in his eyes, and he had flushed, the colour darkening his skin.

'I know you didn't. You were too...occupied.'

'Why didn't you say anything?' he demanded. 'You just—*went*?'

'What was I supposed to say? "Excuse me for intruding"? Or, "Kindly unhand my husband"?'

'You could have asked what the hell we were doing!'

'Why? *That* was perfectly obvious, thanks!'

'Not so obvious as you thought.' The flush was receding. 'Not at all obvious, actually. It was...comfort, that's all. I needed comfort, and Carla's a compassionate woman. And you can take that sneer off your face,' he added sharply. 'It happens to be true.'

Annys wasn't aware that she'd been sneering, but she certainly felt like it. 'Why did you need comfort?' she challenged him.

'Can't you guess?'

He had a pretty good line in sneers himself, Annys thought. 'Because I was pregnant? She was consoling you for *that*?' Anger shook her. How dared he ask another woman for her *compassion* when his wife had just given him the greatest gift a woman could offer to a man? 'And anyway, I don't believe you!' she raged. 'You looked as guilty as hell just now when I told you I'd seen you with her.'

'I wasn't guilty!' Reid said forcefully. And then, on a different note, he added, 'If you want to know, I was embarrassed. I don't habitually cry on a woman's shoulder——'

'It wasn't her *shoulder* you were so interested in——' Annys said acidly.

'All right, then, her bosom!' Reid acknowledged edgily. 'That's what you saw, isn't it? I was at the end of my tether. That morning I could hardly concentrate on what we were supposed to be doing. Carla had worked with me enough to know that something was seriously wrong, and she asked if she could help, offered her sympathy—and I finally let it all out. I'd been going spare trying to save our marriage from the rocks it was heading for, and frantically working all hours in an attempt to get systems into place so that I could be sure the business wouldn't collapse while we sorted our relationship out. I was determined somehow to make you slow down for a while too and put some of the effort into our marriage that you were spending on your career. And then you told me you were pregnant, and I wanted to cheer and shout and toast you in champagne, but that obviously wouldn't have been exactly the thing to do——'

Annys said feebly, 'Why——?'

But he wasn't listening. '—and I was trying to figure out how the hell I could convince you it wasn't going to be the end of the world——'

'What——?'

'And it didn't make any difference, anyway. You went and——' He stopped there and said in stricken tones, 'That's not why you did it, is it?' He shook his head, and said, 'No. You'd planned it, hadn't you? You'd have had to have an appointment.'

'Appointment where?' Annys said, bewildered. 'I don't know what you're talking about!'

'The clinic!' he said impatiently. 'You didn't go and do it just because you'd seen me with Carla, did you? Out of spite, or jealousy? You can't have!'

Her mouth opened in horrified astonishment. 'I didn't! It was an *accident and emergency clinic* I went to, because I fell on the stairs from your office, and when I got home—I'd started to miscarry. Reid, it was an *accident*! That's how I lost the baby.'

Reid swallowed. He was staring at her as though he'd never seen her before. 'You mean, you didn't—it wasn't deliberate?'

'*No!*' She shook her head vehemently, and fought back tears. 'I could never do that to our baby!'

The sudden movement made her feel dizzy, and Reid said, 'You're pale. Come here, you'd better sit down.' He stretched out his hand to her and drew her over to the bed, bending to sweep the papers and folders roughly on to the floor and sit her down against the pillows. 'Put your feet up,' he said, and sat on the edge of the bed, facing her.

'How could you think that?' she asked him indignantly.

'I'm sorry,' he said. 'But you didn't want to have a child in the first place——'

'I what?' Shock upon shock. 'Whatever gave you that idea?'

Reid blinked at her, and frowned. 'You did,' he said curtly. 'The way you told me, you were less than happy about it. I know you wanted to establish your business first, but I hoped——'

'*I* was less than happy?' Annys repeated blankly. 'Reid, I was over the moon, but when I told you about it you just reacted so coolly—you said it was a disaster!'

'No, *you* said that!'

They stared at each other. 'What you said just now,' Annys murmured, 'about wanting to cheer and shout and toast me in champagne. Oh, Reid, why didn't you?' Her eyes suddenly filled with tears, running hotly down her cheeks.

'Annys?' He looked thunderstruck for a second, and then he moved and pulled her roughly into his arms.

'I thought I was being tactful,' he confessed, his face against her hair. 'You didn't seem in a celebratory mood.'

'I had been...earlier,' Annys said, between sobs. 'But it was...a bit anticlimactic...you were so late.'

'I'm sorry about that,' he said belatedly. 'If I'd known——'

'So I tried to be casual instead,' she said, sniffing as she drew away from him a little, wiping her eyes. 'And you thought that meant I didn't like the idea?'

'I thought you were telling me you hated it, that it was going to interfere with your plans for your business. I was trying to talk you into seeing that you could have both a career and a family. We managed to get ourselves into a right mess,' Reid said. He still had his arm about her, but he lifted his other hand and passed a thumb over her wet cheek. 'I've never seen you cry before,' he told her, as though he'd made a wondrous new discovery.

'I'm sorry. I know you don't like it...'

She made to move out of his hold, but he tightened his arm. 'Why do you say that?'

'You hate clinging vines, weak women. You said so. I suppose...your mother——'

'Hang on a minute. What does my mother have to do with this? You never even met her!'

'You said your father felt guilty about her suicide. From what you told me, I guessed she felt she couldn't live without him. You were so adamant that you wanted an independent woman—you didn't want to feel that anyone's happiness hinged on you. But I'm afraid mine does, Reid. I tried not to let it happen, and I promise I'm not going to kill myself, but I haven't been truly happy for five minutes since we parted.'

Reid took her shoulders to hold her away from him so he could see her face. 'I haven't either,' he said. 'Did I make you feel that you couldn't cry on my shoulder if you wanted to? Were you trying to be Superwoman for *my* sake?'

'You admire strong women,' Annys said.

'I admire *you*! I *love* you! If you wept all over me ten times a day I wouldn't care——'

Annys grinned suddenly. 'You'd hate it!' she accused him.

'Well, maybe. But so long as you were doing it on *my* shoulder I could stand it. You see, my happiness depends on you, Annys. If I didn't know it before, I've certainly found that out in the last three years. Only I thought the most important thing for you was your career, your business. You put so much energy into it, there seemed damn all left for me. And for any children.' He paused. 'Do I take it that this baby is wanted, even though it was unplanned?'

'I wouldn't give this baby up for anything!' she said, looking down. 'I never did stop mourning the other one.'

'Neither did I. I tried not to be angry with you for what I thought you'd done, but I couldn't help it. And I grieved for that child.'

'We should have grieved together,' she said, looking up at him, this time not trying to hide the tears.

'Yes,' Reid agreed huskily. Tears glittering in his own eyes, he took her in his arms again.

Some time later they lay together on the bed, Annys's damp cheek against his chest.

'That's why Carla was holding you that day?' she said. 'For comfort?'

'I told you, yes. I was deathly afraid our marriage was foundering, and I thought you resented the baby. Carla's a good friend.'

Annys tamped down a quite unreasoning resentment that he'd gone to Carla for comfort that he had never asked of her. She ought to be glad that he'd had someone.

'She's happily married, by the way,' Reid went on, 'with children of her own. I like her, but not as a lover. I've never looked at another woman since you came into my life.'

Annys raised her head and gave him a level stare, and he grinned. 'Well, hardly. And looking isn't a crime.' The smile fading, he said, 'Seriously, Annys. I don't know how I can convince you. But I also don't know why you should doubt my word.'

Annys bit her lip. 'In a way my parents were right. We got married so soon, I hadn't had time to get to know you, to know that I could trust you. For ages I'd been jealous for no reason, thinking maybe you were seeing other women when you were away from me——'

Reid gave a startled exclamation. 'You thought—why didn't you *say*?'

'I despised myself for it. How could I say anything when all I had to go on was unfounded suspicion? I didn't want you to know how insecure I felt, and I suppose I didn't want to start acting like a woman who couldn't bear to let her husband out of her sight. You'd have been furious, and with good reason. You told me that you didn't want a little woman waiting at home for you. A *jealous* little woman would have been the end! Then, when I saw you with Carla...'

'I suppose it did look pretty compromising,' he said, 'but I'd have expected you to come in with guns blazing, rather than run away and say nothing.'

'Maybe you didn't know me very well, either.'

'Tell me about the you I don't know.'

Annys hesitated. 'You always said I could do anything, that I was strong.'

'No one can be strong all the time.'

'No. But I thought I had to be. My parents were in their forties when I was born, and I think they had this idea that they might not always be around to look out for me, so I had to be able to make my own security. They were very keen for me to go to university, to have a good steady job. At least until I got married. Something to fall back on, my mother used to say. I always felt I had to do well for their sakes. And when my dad was made redundant I decided that I was never going to be at someone else's mercy. I wanted to rely on myself alone. That's why I was so touchy, I suppose, when you offered to help.'

'Mmm, you were, rather.'

'I guess all that drive and ambition you so admire is founded on fear, really.'

'Not on a desire to do something well, on the satisfaction of seeing your work used and appreciated?'

'That too,' Annys admitted. 'But I can have that without operating a world-wide empire. Since I've been pregnant again, I don't feel quite so committed to expanding the business.'

'Want to concentrate on what's expanding your waistline for a while?'

She laughed. 'Yes. A different kind of creation. I don't want to lose this baby,' she added soberly. 'The doctor says it's OK to carry on with my normal activities, so long as I don't get too tired. But I told Kate I'm going to change things a bit, delegate more.'

'That's hard for you.'

'I'll learn. You did, didn't you?'

'Yep. Some things can't be delegated, though.'

'Such as?'

'Well,' Reid said. He turned her gently on the bed so that he was above her. 'This, for instance.' He bent his head to kiss her lips. 'What did the doctor say,' he asked her, 'about this kind of activity?'

'Making love with a man who's not my husband, you mean?' Annys asked innocently.

'I am your husband, in every way that matters.'

'Legally——'

'Legally nothing. I'm the only husband you're ever going to have, so you may as well get used to the idea. We can fix up the legal details later.'

'Well, in that case, and if you promise to make it legal—again—she said that it's quite OK.'

'Good.' His lips were wandering over her face, one hand stroking her breast.

'Of course,' Annys said as he nestled closer to her, 'I told her the question didn't arise.'

'The question just did.'

'Mmm. I noticed something had...' She looked at him from under lowered lids, a teasing smile on her face.

Reid laughed. 'We missed a great opportunity,' he told her, his fingers finding a button on her blouse and flicking it open.

'We did?'

'We could have had a second honeymoon, on board Toroa, if we hadn't been so busy competing with each other to see who was the fastest, strongest, bravest...'

'And if you hadn't been so busy hovering around the gorgeous Xianthe,' Annys told him, her eyes gleaming with remembered jealousy.

'Gorgeous, is she?' Reid said. 'Never noticed,' he lied blandly.

Annys made to hit him, and he caught her wrist and bore it back down to the pillows, his lips trailing from there down the inside of her arm to the elbow before wandering to her neck. 'Anyway,' he said, his voice muffled. 'What about you and that slimeball, Tancred?'

'He is not a slimeball! He's just ... an incorrigible, incurable male chauvinist.'

Reid grunted. 'So why did you encourage him to hang around you? I wanted to kill him.'

'I didn't. He was just there. Why did you encourage Xianthe? You might have hurt her badly, you know.'

He lifted his head for a moment. 'Rot. I'm much too old for her. And she knew I couldn't take my eyes off you for a minute. I spent time with her because besides being a nice girl she was the weak link in our team, and I wanted to bring her up to scratch.'

'Determined to beat me, weren't you?'

'Yep. As much as you were to beat me.'

'Why did we do it?' Annys asked. 'It all looks positively childish now.'

'Guess so,' he agreed. 'We're competitive people, you and I. We'll need to watch that, especially with our kids. We don't want them to grow up thinking that winning is the only important thing—do we?'

'No.' Annys shook her head. 'We never talked about how we would want to bring up our children.'

'We never talked about anything much,' Reid agreed. He had undone all her buttons to the waist, and slipped his hand inside, caressing her warm skin. 'That was one of our problems, I guess. Our communication skills on this level were so good, we never bothered a great deal with other ways of communicating.'

Annys thought about that while she traced a slow line down the middle of his bared chest, watching it with silent absorption. 'You're right,' she said. 'We should talk.' She took her finger away and raised her eyes to his face.

Reid looked resigned. He removed his hand from the firmly rounded breast where he had just found an interesting hardness in the centre and said, 'Now?'

'We-ell...' Annys said, giving him an earnest stare. 'I mean, we have a lot to decide on, and plan for. Don't you think...?'

'No, actually——'

'Don't you think...' Annys's hand went to the buckle on his belt '...that later would be a good time?'

POSTCARDS FROM EUROPE

HARLEQUIN PRESENTS.

Travel across Europe in 1994 with Harlequin Presents. Collect a new Postcards from Europe title each month!

Don't miss
ROMAN SPRING
by Sandra Marton
Harlequin Presents #1660

Available in June wherever
Harlequin Presents books are sold.

HPPFE6

Hi,

Italy, as always, is a model's paradise. But I'm tired of the obligatory parties, the devouring eyes. Particularly those of Nicolo Sabatini, who seems to think I should be for his eyes only.

Love, Caroline